Neighbours 5

Married at last – at long last. A miracle had been wrought. Des still couldn't believe it. 'You may kiss me now,' Daphne had said, clutching her bouquet.

'I know,' Des had said with a sheepish smile while everyone looked on with beams of approval – and perhaps relief. 'It's been a long wait.'

Deep down, no one – Des probably more than anyone else – had believed it would happen. Surely the bad luck that had dogged him in the past would once more reassert itself at the last minute. But no, this time it had all been carried off with the utmost smoothness. There had been no standing around at the altar in a cold sweat while the clergyman kept glancing at his wristwatch and the congregation shifted uneasily in their pews; there had been no sinking feeling that came with the realisation that once again he had been left in the lurch. Four times it had happened before; it was a sensation with which he had become familiar. He gazed fondly at his new wife. Was it really true? Was it just a dream from which he was about to be brutally awakened?

Also by Carl Ruhen and available in Star Books

NEIGHBOURS 5

Carl Ruhen

From an original concept by Reg Watson and based on the scripts of Ginny Lowndes, Cheredith Mok, Sally Webb, Roger Moulton, David Phillips, Peter Connah, Reg Watson, Adrian van den Bok, John Upton, Ray Harding, Phillip Ryall, Nicholas Langton, Christine Schofield, Christine McCourt, Penny Fraser, Jill James, Rick Maier, Ysabelle Dean, John Linton, Dave Worthington, Ray Kolle, Greg Stevens, Lois Booton, Christine Stanton, Bill Searle, Greg Millin, Betty Quin.

A STAR BOOK
published by
the Paperback Division of
W.H. Allen & Co. Plc

A Star Book
Published in 1988
by the Paperback Division of
W.H. Allen & Co. Plc
44 Hill Street, London W1X 8LB

Copyright © Horwitz Grahame Pty Ltd, 1988

ISBN 0 352 322853

One

'I want to go on the pill,' Charlene said. She had blurted it out at last.

Clive Gibbons stared at her blankly for a moment, then sighed. 'You'd better come inside, and we'll talk about it.'

Charlene was very nervous; she also sensed defeat. Perhaps it had been a mistake to come here after all. 'Look, maybe I should leave it,' she said hurriedly. 'If I come in I'll be late for school. Then I'll be in trouble.'

Clive eyed her shrewdly. 'And if you don't you could be in worse trouble – am I right or wrong?'

'I don't know.'

He held the front door open. 'It sounds important. It's got to be worth five minutes.'

She had come to him because he was a doctor – or had been a doctor. Now he was a bum with a medical degree. 'Well . . . ' She thought quickly. She had come so far, had blurted out her wish to go on the pill. She was doing this for Scott. 'I suppose so,' she said reluctantly.

She followed him into the house. In the kitchen, Daphne Lawrence, still in her dressing gown, was drinking coffee. 'A visitor,' Clive announced.

'So I see. Hi, Lennie.'

'Hi.'

Charlene's awkwardness probably showed. Daphne certainly sensed something. She turned to Clive. 'Would you like me to make myself scarce?'

Clive was looking at Charlene. 'It's up to you, Lennie,' he said.

Charlene thought about it. Perhaps it would be better, she decided, if Daphne *were* there. Daphne was a woman; she would be sympathetic. 'That's all right,' she said.

'Fine. Take a seat.' Charlene perched herself on the edge of a chair. If only she didn't feel so gangly in her school uniform. 'Charlene wants to go on the pill,' Clive explained to Daphne. 'She wants me to give her a prescription.' He turned back to Charlene. 'But unfortunately I can't.'

The resentment flooded back. 'I might have guessed you wouldn't,' she said accusingly.

'Now hang on, wait a minute.' Clive was holding up one hand. 'It's not like that at all. It's just that I'm not practising at the moment and I don't have the facilities I would need to give you a complete check-up. But the Family Planning Centre does – so I suggest you go to them.'

'Why do I need a check-up? All I want is the pill.'

'Yes, but there are different types,' Clive informed her, 'and they all have different hormone levels. A pill that is suitable for someone else might be totally wrong for you.'

'Oh.' Charlene had had no idea. She had thought it would be a very simple matter.

'And that's where the Family Planning Centre can help,' Clive went on. 'You don't have to worry about going along to see them. You'll find

2

that they're very helpful – and they won't insist on lecturing you about what is right and what is wrong. I mean, adopt a moral attitude. You'll find them very relaxed and friendly.'

Well, if it was as simple as he made it sound . . . 'I suppose I *could* go and see them,' she said thoughtfully.

'But you shouldn't leave it too late,' Clive suggested. 'If you *do* go on the pill – and that's a big if – you won't be one hundred percent protected for the first month.'

'A whole *month*?' Charlene was dismayed. That was a long time. So it wasn't exactly as simple as taking an aspirin after all; it was becoming quite a complicated business. 'Isn't there something else I could use that would be just as safe?'

'Sure there is,' Clive replied. 'But at this stage I think you'll find that the pill is the easiest approach.'

Daphne put down her coffee cup. 'Why don't you talk it over with your boyfriend?' she suggested. 'It's his problem, too, you know.'

'Oh, I couldn't.'

'Why not?'

Charlene felt uncomfortably that she was getting deeper and deeper into this thing. She was beginning to feel quite depressed. 'Oh, it's hard to talk about these things,' she murmured, looking down at the table.

'But if you can't even talk about it,' Clive said, 'are you sure you're ready to take it further?'

Charlene wasn't sure about anything any more. It was Scott who was putting on the pressure. He

3

was the one who was being so insistent about all this – and she did love him, there was no doubt about that much at least. She shrugged her shoulders and continued to stare down at the table. 'Well . . . '

'The people at the Centre are used to seeing, well, couples together,' Clive said gently. 'They won't moralise. It will all be quite confidential.'

Charlene looked up at him.' And they won't tell Mum?'

Clive shook his head. 'Or anyone else. They figure it's entirely your own business – which it is, of course. And by the way,' he added, 'you have the same guarantee from Daphne and me.' Daphne nodded in confirmation of this.

'Thanks.' Charlene smiled bleakly at them both. She thought about Clive's suggestion. Perhaps there was some wisdom in that; it was only right that Scott should be involved from the outset: The burden of decision did need to be shared. 'All right then,' she said at last. 'I'll talk it over with him. I'll ask him to come with me to the Centre.' She rose to her feet; she was feeling a little better now that she had made up her mind to do this. 'Thanks for – you know. I would have spoken to Mum about it, but all I would have got was a lecture.' Her mother would have been down on her like a ton of bricks: Sometimes Charlene felt that her mother had no appreciation of the needs and concerns of a seventeen-year-old girl. 'I'll see you then.'

'Good luck,Lennie' Clive said as she headed for the door.

As she emerged from the house, Charlene saw

that Nikki Dennison was waiting for her. 'Oh, I'm sorry. I didn't know you were there.'

'That's all right.' They began to walk along the street together. 'What were you doing in there?' Nikki asked.

'Ah, no reason,' Charlene answered evasively. 'I was just saying hello.'

Nikki glanced at her suspiciously. 'Before school?'

'I wanted to talk to Clive about something.'

'Like what?'

'Nothing important.'

But Nikki wasn't about to give up as easily as that. She was on the trail of something that could prove interesting. 'Come on, Lennie. You can tell me.'

'Oh well, Charlene thought in resignation, why not? Nikki was her friend, and frankly, Charlene still did feel the need to confide in someone about what she proposed to do. She took a deep breath. 'I asked him to put me on the pill.'

As she expected, Nikki was horrified. 'You didn't!' She exclaimed.

'So what if I did?' Charlene returned defiantly 'It doesn't make any difference, anyway. He wouldn't do it.'

'That's all right then,' Nikki said in obvious relief. 'I don't know how you can even *think* about it.'

'It's better than getting pregnant,' Charlene retorted.

'But why do you have to do it at all?'

Charlene was becoming infuriated by her friend's

attitude. She was already beginning to regret having told her; she should have realised that Nikki would adopt this holier-than-thou attitude. 'Because I want to, and Scott wants to, and if I don't . . . '

'You think he'll dump you,' Nikki finished for her. 'But you don't know that for sure, do you? And, anyway, if he does, then you'll know that he was only after the one thing. And good riddance.'

'But he isn't,' Charlene cried angrily. 'He loves me, and there's nothing wrong with sleeping with someone if you love them.'

They turned a corner. The school was ahead of them. 'Lennie, I'm your friend,' Nikki said placatingly. 'But you have to think. I mean, what will your mother say? And you know what the girls at school will call you.' Charlene had heard enough; she quickened her pace. 'They'll call you a slut, Lennie.'

Charlene kept walking rapidly, her head down and full of determination. She didn't want to talk about it any more. 'Lennie?' Nikki called after her in a puzzled voice. 'Lennie, wait for me.'

When she told Scott what had happened that morning, and suggested he come with her to the Family Planning Centre, he refused outright. 'There's no way you're going to catch me in one of those places,' he said.

'But we have to,' Charlene insisted. 'I don't want anything to happen.'

Scott sat beside her on the park bench, staring out across the lake. 'And *I* don't want anything to happen either,' he muttered. 'But I'm not going to one of those centres. I'll take care of it.'

'How?'

'Just leave it to me,' Scott said confidently. 'I know what to do.'

Looking at him, Charlene wondered if he did.

When she arrived home from school, her mother took her to one side. She wanted a word, she said, and there was something quite serious in her manner that made Charlene a little apprehensive as she followed her mother into the living room of the Ramsay house where they were staying.

'I don't want either of us to raise our voices,' Madge Mitchell began after they had settled down on the sofa. 'But we do have to have a little chat about your behaviour.'

'If you're talking about Scott,' Charlene said resentfully, 'Why don't you just come right out and say so?'

'Yes, all right then, Madge said uncomfortably. Possibly she thought that this was not going to be as easy as she had anticipated. 'Since you brought his name up, we may as well start our discussion there. You see, it's obvious to me that you're becoming far too serious.'

Charlene had been half-expecting something like this from the time her mother had caught her and Scott on this very same sofa when she had come home unexpectedly early one afternoon. It had been quite a passionate scene that had confronted her. 'So?'

'Even if *you* can't see the dangers,'Madge said, 'I most certainly can. And as your mother I can't possibly allow it to go on.'

As if she had committed some great crime, Charlene thought bitterly. She *was* seventeen after all; she was already a young woman with her own life to lead. And she was in love. 'You don't know what it's like, Mum,' she said resentfully. 'I love Scott.'

Madge's face hardened. 'Charlene, don't cheapen the word.'

'I'm *not*,' Charlene cried vehemently. 'He loves me, too.'

Madge shook her head decisively . 'He'll use you, and discard you. I can already see it happening.'

Charlene had a sudden suspicion. Her eyes narrowed. 'You've been talking to Clive, haven't you?'

Madge looked startled. 'Yes, I have. But I fail to see . . . '

'It's not fair.' Charlene sprang to her feet. She was very angry. Clive had *promised*. 'I can't trust *anyone*,' she cried, tears of frustration pricking in her eyes. 'And I'm not going to listen to any more of your lectures, either.' She moved rapidly to the door.

'Charlene'

'Forget it, Mum.'

When Scott told her he had managed to borrow the key to Paul's room at Lassiter's Hotel where he had been living since he left home, Charlene realised, with mingled apprehension and anticipation that, the time had now come for her to prove her love with him. And once again, she wondered if they were doing the right thing. She had to trust Scott. He had told her that he knew what to do, but all the same.

Her nervousness increased as Scott unlocked the door of his brother's hotel room, then with a little bow, ushered her ahead of him. He closed and put up the chain in the door behind them. They were alone in the room.

'I love you, Lennie.'

'I love you, too.'

They were on the bed. He was kissing her. Although she was beginning to respond to his embraces, she was still holding back a little. 'Don't worry,' he said with a smile. We're doing the right thing.'

'I know.' But she still wasn't totally convinced. She looked searchingly into his eyes. 'Tell me something.'

'Tell you what?'

'If you've ever been with anyone else. You know – like this – all the way.'

Scott was clearly taken aback by the question. 'Well . . . ' Then he smiled rather self-confidently. 'Yes, sure,' he said with a touch of bravado. 'Only a few though. They didn't mean anything.'

Charlene sat up stiffly. She turned her head away from him. 'And that's what you'll say about me. That I didn't mean anything.'

'Hey, listen. He placed a hand on her shoulder. 'No, you're twisting what I said. It's not the same with you. I mean, it's different. I don't know. They weren't as important to me.' He gently squeezed her shoulder.

Charlene turned back to face him. '*Am* I important?'

'Of course you are.' Scott was staring at her

intently. He spoke quickly and with apparent sincerity. 'You know you are.' He hesitated. 'Why? Have *you* been with anyone else?'

'Only one.' That had been in Coffs Harbour. It seemed ages ago.

'Oh.' Now it was Scott's turn to stiffen and pull away, to be disappointed as she had been disappointed. 'Are you serious?'

Charlene nodded. 'And it wasn't something casual.' She sighed. The memories were still fresh, still bitter. 'I really loved him – and I thought he loved me, too.'

'Then why didn't you tell me this before?' Scott demanded.

Charlene was suddenly confused. She didn't know what was the matter with him. He had made his confession, and she had made hers. He was angry, but she wasn't. She was a little sad, that was all. 'Does it matter?'

'Yes, of course it does.'

Why? How? What was the difference? Suddenly, Charlene found herself on the defensive. 'There was only one, Scott,' she said unhappily. 'Just the one. And I loved him.' And how true that was — what a fool she had been. 'And what about you? I'm not *your* first — you just told me so.'

'Yeah, but that's different.'

Charlene still couldn't see how it was different. 'Why is it different?'

Scott pushed himself up from the bed. 'It's just different, that's all,' he muttered.

'But, Scott.'

He crossed the room to the door. He took

off the chain, then opened the door. Confused and miserable, and with everything now in tatters, Charlene stared at the door for a long time after it had closed behind him.

It was all over; she vowed never to see him again. But because they lived next door to each other, it was inevitable that she *would* see him again – over and over again. She didn't know how she would react to that. She thought very seriously of returning to Coffs Harbour. She could move back in with her father, and Susan who was now expecting his baby. She had always got along quite well with Susan.

That night, she was unable to sleep. She tossed and turned and stared up at the ceiling and the faint wash of light that filtered in around the edges of the curtains from the street outside. She could hear distant traffic.

She thought of Coffs Harbour with its fishing boats and motels. She thought of Greg with whom, once, she had believed she was in love. But most of all she thought about Scott and what had happened that afternoon in the hotel room. And the more she thought about him, and the way he had behaved, the more angry she became. He had left her there, humiliated and feeling somehow grubby – and he'd had no right to do that. He had behaved like a thorough pig. Charlene fumed and clenched her fists; she groaned and wept in rage and frustration; she felt like screaming. No, she decided, he wouldn't be allowed to get away with it.

'Hey, Lennie, wait a minute. I want to talk to you.'

She had seen him as she came out of the house. He was the first person she had seen, and she'd had the impression that he was waiting for her. She had turned quickly away. She had heard rapid footsteps behind her; she had walked faster. 'Hey, Lennie!'

She stopped, but didn't turn back to face him. She stood rigidly. 'I'm not interested,' she said in a strained voice. 'Okay?'

'But it's important.' There was a pleading note in his voice. 'It's about yesterday. I just wanted to say I'm sorry. The way I treated you. I was upset. I didn't know what I was doing.'

'And I've got something to say to you, too, Scott.'

If Scott hadn't known what he was doing yesterday, Charlene knew what she was doing right now – and it gave her the greatest satisfaction to do it. The strength surged into her as, suddenly pivoting on the footpath outside the Robinson home, she slammed her fist against his jaw in a punch that must have come down from the clouds on this fine sunny morning. His mouth gaping in astonishment, Scott reeled backwards from the force of the blow. He lost his balance and fell. Charlene was already beginning to feel much better.

Two

Zoe Davis was pregnant, and it seemed that the last person to find out about it was her father himself – and even then Jim Robinson had discovered it only by accident. Andrea had let it slip when Jim had stormed next door to remonstrate with her about her son Bradley's latest atrocity. (This time it was the mangling of his dead wife's wedding ring with a knife in an attempt to make it smaller so that it would fit Lucy's finger, the two of them having recently decided to become engaged, notwithstanding their tender years.) Andrea had stoutly defended her son, as she always did when one or another of the neighbours had the temerity to complain about his behaviour. There had been quite a lot of yelling. Jim had lost his temper. He had accused Andrea of being an irresponsible parent.

'Irresponsible?' Andrea had laughed quite unpleasantly. 'What would *you* know about that? And, anyway, why don't you run your own life properly before you start telling other people how to run theirs? What sort of man your age would be careless enough to get a girl pregnant?'

And that was how Jim had come to learn that he was about to become a father.

'We'll have to get married,' Jim said earnestly. 'You can't bring up a child on your own.'

'Lots of women do, Zoe calmly pointed out to him. 'Look at Andrea.'

Jim grimaced. 'And then look at Bradley.'

'She spoils him. I won't make that mistake.'

Zoe had needed time and space, she had said, to think about her relationship with Jim and put it in its proper perspective. She had gone to the mountains where she had done a lot of walking, breathing the crisp mountain air and sleeping well at nights. Now she was back, staying once more in Des Clarke's house with Des, Andrea and the obnoxious little Bradley. Jim had missed her terribly.

'But you don't have to face it on your own,' he said now. 'Having the child is just another good reason why we should get married.'

They had been over this many times before. Zoe siged. 'It doesn't work that way, Jim.'

They were seated at a corner table in the Waterhole Bar of Lassiter's Hotel. Jim was drinking beer while Zoe sipped a mineral water. She hadn't wanted to come with him at first. She had told him there was little point; she had made up her mind during those long mountain walks that there was no future in their relationship. But Jim had been insistent, and she had finally agreed to come.

'But all you were worried about, if we got married, was how I would feel about having more kids.' Jim gave her a wry smile. 'Now it looks as though that decision has been taken out of our hands. So – he spread his hands – ' Let's just make the best of it.'

'But what about all the other problems?' Zoe queried. 'The hassles with your family? The age difference between us?'

'She was just being stubborn, that was all. She was finding difficulties where they didn't really exist. Jim gestured impatiently. 'We could get around all that if you would just give it a chance.'

'It wouldn't work,' Zoe said adamantly.

Trying not to give vent to his exasperation, Jim spoke quietly and deliberately. 'The child is entitled to a decent start in life, which means a proper home and two parents. So what's the alternative? You trying to cope on your own?'

'It's better than getting married for all the wrong reasons.' She shook her head. 'No, Jim, I'm not going to change my mind – and that's final.'

That evening, after Lucy and Scott had gone to bed, Jim discussed the problem with his mother-in-law. He was disappointed because Lucy hadn't come to him to say good night. Of course, she knew about Zoe's condition. Bradley had made sure of that – yet another black mark against him.

'Well, she's not sure of you at the moment,' Helen Daniels explained. 'She's afraid that the new baby will replace her in your affections.'

Jim laughed bitterly. 'She's got nothing to worry about on that score,' he said. 'Zoe's determined that I'm not even going to lay eyes on the baby.'

Helen began to put the dinner dishes away. 'Is that why you were so desperate to marry her?'

I love her,' Jim said forcefully. 'You know that.'

15

'Yes, but you accepted her decision until you learnt that she was pregnant.'

'The child comes first.'

Helen closed the cupboard door, then turned to face him squarely. 'Jim, if there are troubles in a marriage,' she said quietly, 'it's wrong to use the children to try to hold it together. And that's what you'd be doing.'

'I'm the child's father,' Jim reminded her tautly. 'Surely that entitles me to ⸱ ⸱ rights?'

'But you can't *force* her to marry you,' Helen pointed out to him. 'Ultimately, the decision will have to be hers. The most you can do is wait quietly in the wings and see what happens.'

And that was just what Jim was not prepared to do. 'I'm damned if I will,' he snapped. 'Whether she likes it or not, I'm definitely going to have a say in that child's upbringing.'

It was with this resolution in mind that he decided to have it out with Zoe there and then. Des Clarke opened the front door to him. 'Oh, she's not here,' he said when Jim told him he had come to see Zoe. 'She's having dinner at Clive's.'

'I'll go there, then.' Jim turned away.

'No, Jim, wait.' Des grasped his shoulder. 'Why don't you wait for her here?'

'No.'

But Des, holding him by the arm now, was guiding him into the hall. 'There's no point in making a scene in front of everybody. Just come in and wait for her. Then you can talk to her privately.'

Reluctantly, Jim allowed himself to be led into the house. Des closed the door behind them, then gestured towards the living room.

'I don't know, Des,' Jim said helplessly when they were seated opposite each other. 'It's our problem, and we should be facing it together. But it seems she doesn't want to have anything to do with me.'

'She just needs time,' Des offered sympathetically.

'She can have all the time in the world,' Jim said. 'As long as she doesn't do anything stupid.' This was something else that had been worrying him: another alternative that was always available to Zoe.

'Like what?' Des was regarding him quizzically.

'Like not going through with the pregnancy,' Jim replied. 'I mean, I would hate the baby . . . well, not to have a chance in the world.'

Des shook his head. 'Zoe wouldn't do that. No way.'

'But what *will* she do? Have it adopted?'

'I don't think Zoe's had much time to think about it.'

'But what is there to think about? 'Jim persisted. 'The two of us – we can raise the baby together. As any two parents would. As it should be.' He looked steadily at Des. 'But she won't even listen to me? Why, Des? Why won't she listen to me?'

Des was unable to supply him with an answer. Jim stood up. 'I'd better go.'

'She won't be long.'

'No. I'll catch up with her later.'

He caught up with her early the following morning. 'It's too late, Jim,' she said.

'What do you mean?'

'Just that. It's too late.'

Jim couldn't believe what he was hearing. 'I love you, Zoe – and despite what you say I know you love me.'

'Not any more.'

'Zoe!'

Zoe shook her head sorrowfully. 'I was crazy to think it could have worked. But there were just too many obstacles.

'Nothing we couldn't have overcome,' Jim said miserably.

'Don't you understand, Jim? I'm not interested any more. I don't want to even try.'

'But, Zoe . . . ' Jim stared at her bleakly. 'You don't mean this.'

Zoe turned away from him. She was in her dressing-gown. 'Maybe things could have been different,' she said distantly, 'if your family had approved of me. There were just too many hassles.'

She was being totally unfair. Things would have worked out in time – just a little time. Of course, there were adjustments to be made. Stepping close to her, Jim reached for her hand. 'Zoe.'

She pulled her hand away. 'And I won't be forced into anything because of the baby,' she said tightly. 'If you want to help support it, then okay, maybe that's something we can work out when we get closer to the time.'

'But that's not satisfactory to me,' Jim said tersely. 'The child should have a proper family.'

She rounded on him. He could see she was angry. Her cheeks had reddened and her eyes were hard. 'Why don't you stop hassling me?' she cried. 'Because if you don't, I'll have to leave, and then you'll never see me *or* the baby again.' Holding the dressing-gown tightly around her, Zoe backed away from him. 'Just get out of my life, Jim. I mean it. I've had enough. I don't want to be bothered any more.'

Jim was sure she didn't really mean it. She was overwrought, that was all; she was under a tremendous strain; she needed a little time. She would come good again with a little time. She would listen to him then and realise that what he had to say made excellent sense.

The following evening, after he had returned home from work, he decided to try again. Maybe she was feeling better now, he thought as he walked towards Des Clarke's house. Maybe now she would listen to him.

A car pulled up beside him. 'She's not there, Dad.'

With growing alarm, he moved around quickly to the driver's side. 'Where is she?'

'Gone,' Paul told him, simply.

Jim glared at his older son who had also done his utmost to put a spoke in the relationship. 'What do you mean – gone? Gone where?'

Paul stared back at his father levelly. 'She got sick of you giving her a hard time.'

'Where is she, Paul?'

19

Paul said nothing. He had turned his head away.

'You know where she is, don't you?' Jim urged.

'Just forget it, Dad,' Paul said quietly. 'She doesn't want to see you.'

Jim was only just managing to resist the urge to grab his son, haul him out of the car and shake the truth out of him. Of course Paul would have had something to do with this – Zoe was his secretary. Paul would have arranged something; he would have done anything to ensure that they stayed apart. Savagely, in his frustration, Jim banged his fist down on the roof of the car. 'She's having my baby,' he shouted. 'I have a *right* to know.'

'Yes, I do know where she is.' Paul was looking back up at his father again. He spoke angrily. 'But I'm not going to tell you. She's somewhere where you won't be able to hassle her.'

He had to live with it; Zoe needed more time; she had gone away. Jim was quite unbearable for the next few days.

It was Paul who brought the news that afternoon about two weeks later. Helen had just made some sandwiches for lunch when he arrived, looking quite tense about something. 'Oh, you're just in time for something to eat,' she greeted him.

'No thanks, Gran,' Paul said grimly. 'I've got to get back to the office.' He turned to his father who was sitting at the kitchen table. 'Dad, I've got some bad news.'

Jim frowned up at him. 'The business?'

'No. It's Zoe. She's in hospital. Dad . . . She's lost the baby.'

'*What?*' Jim leapt to his feet.

'She had an ectopic pregnancy. They had to operate.'

'For God's sake, Paul, talk sense will you.'

Paul began to explain. Zoe had been found unconscious on the floor of the flat where he had suggested she stay for a while until its owner, a friend of Paul's, returned from his holiday. She had been rushed to hospital, luckily just in time. It seemed that the foetus had lodged inside the fallopian tubes, and as it had grown the tube had expanded until it had finally burst. The pain must have been terrible. They had operated on her immediately - and of course there was no way the baby could be saved. It had been touch and go there for a while.

Jim was horrified. 'I'd better go and see her.'

'No, Dad, you can't,' Paul said sombrely. 'She has already said she doesn't want to see you – so why make things more difficult?'

'But I can't just pretend I don't *care*. Not now.'

'Let's face it, Dad. It's over. Her losing the baby doesn't change that.'

Jim was unable to comprehend this. 'What am I supposed to do? Ignore it?'

'For her sake, yes,' Paul replied. 'Maybe it's a blessing in some ways.'

Anger sparked in Jim. Helen reproached her grandson. 'Paul, that's a terrible thing to say.'

Paul gestured ruefully. 'I'm sorry, Gran, but *somebody* has to make Dad understand.' He turned back to his father. 'Zoe's going to be much better off when you stop hassling her,' he said brutally.

Jim was only just getting over the first shock of what had happened. Now he was shocked again. He slumped back onto the chair. 'I'll talk to you later,' Paul said to Helen as he moved to the door.'

'It was my baby, too,' Jim groaned after he had gone. 'Aren't *I* supposed to feel anything?'

'Of course you are,' Helen said sympathetically.

He looked up at her bleakly. 'The worst of it is that Paul is probably right,' he said. 'I probably shouldn't go and see her. But I'm damned if I can just sit here and do nothing.'

'I know,' Helen said gently.

Daphne Lawrence was sitting with Zoe in her hospital room when Jim arrived with an enormous bunch of flowers. Zoe was looking very pale; she obviously wasn't pleased to see him. 'I brought you some flowers,' he said awkwardly, holding them out to her.

'I know,' she said listlessly. 'Thank you. They're lovely.'

Not knowing what else to do with them, he placed them on the table beside her bed. There were a number of crumpled tissues on the table and Zoe's eyes were red-rimmed.

'Paul told me what happened,' Jim said. 'I'm dreadfully sorry.'

Zoe shrugged. Her face was expressionless. 'You and me both.'

There was an uncomfortable silence. Jim glanced at Daphne, but saw no reassurance there. 'He also said that I shouldn't come and see you. But I had to come.'

Zoe's face was still blank. Daphne shifted on her chair. 'Zoe?'

'No, you go, Daphne,' Zoe said with a slight wave of her hand. 'You can't leave the coffee shop forever.'

Rising from the chair, Daphne leaned over the bed and kissed Zoe's cheek. 'I'll come back tonight.'

Zoe smiled wanly. 'Okay.'

With a nod to Jim, Daphne left the room. Still hovering by the side of the bed, Jim looked down at Zoe with an expression of concern. 'Are you all right?' he asked.

'No.' Zoe's eyes were brimming. She reached for another tissue from the almost empty box beside the flowers Jim had brought.

'Is there anything I can do?'

Zoe dabbed at her eyes with the tissue. 'I don't know if anyone has told you,' she said weakly, 'but it's . . . probable that I won't be able to have any more children. Oh . . . I'll cope with that eventually, I suppose, but right now it's a little hard to take.'

Jim lowered himself on to the edge of the bed. He reached for her hand. This time she made no attempt to withdraw it. They sat in silence for a few moments. Zoe dropped the crumpled tissue onto the table. 'I wish I could help,' Jim murmured. 'I know I can't', but I just wish I could.'

Her hand was lifeless in his own. When she spoke her voice sounded as if it were coming from very far away. 'You can stop showing me how much you still need me.'

Jim smiled briefly. 'I didn't know it was so obvious.'

'It's not that I don't still feel a million things for you,' Zoe said sadly, 'because I do. But I've thought about it every which way, and no matter how I work it out I still can't see any happy future for us.' She regarded him intently with large and sorrowful eyes. 'It's over, Jim. You'll only hurt me more if you won't accept that.'

Jim held her hand in his own. Gently, he began to stroke it. 'If that's the way you want it.'

'It is, Jim.'

There was a faint stinging sensation in his eyes, a constriction in his throat. Yes, it was the end – he could see that now. 'I, I'll always care for you, Zoe,' he said unevenly. 'Nothing can ever change that. Nothing.'

Three

There they were, in groups or alone, lying on towels spread out on the sand and soaking up the sun, reading books or languorously rubbing sun lotion into their skin, talking, laughing, squinting into the sun, running along the sand, walking along the sand, diving under the waves, riding the waves, shaking the water out of their hair, drying their hair. There were girls everywhere.

'Let's check 'em out, eh?' Scott suggested.

Mike grinned at him. 'Shall I tell Lennie, or will you?'

'Aw come on, mate, a guy can have a look.'

And there was certainly plenty to look at, Mike decided as they trudged up the sand from the water's edge with their boards under their arms. The surf pounded relentlessly behind them. Seagulls wheeled in lazy circles above them. The sand crunched gently beneath their feet. Everything sparkled under a brilliant sun.

'Yeah,' Mike said with a nod. 'I think I might do a bit more than have a look, myself.'

'What about Nikki?'

Nikki was miles away, back in Erinsborough. This wasn't a time to be thinking about Nikki. 'Come on, mate,' Mike said incredulously. 'We're on holiday. Got to relax.'

Strictly speaking, they weren't on holiday. They were in training for the school diving championship, which this year was being held on the narrow but crowded isthmus between ocean and harbour across which, during the summer months, the ferries transported the holiday-makers in their droves from the city. Mike had only just been selected for the school team; Scott was on the reserve. They would be here for a week, staying with the rest of the team in one of the motels that linked the beachfront.

'And that's where you could start,' Scott said, pointing to a girl in a wetsuit who was studying to keep a board from slipping out beneath her arm as she headed towards the surf.

The wetsuit clung tightly to the slender contours of her body. Her hair was blonde, her skin deeply tanned. Mike stared at her, then shook his head doubtfully. 'Naaah.'

'Go on,' Scott urged him. 'I'll come, too.' They had only just reached their towels where they had left them on the sand. Scott was on his feet again. 'Come on.' He moved off down the sand to intercept the girl, who was still having trouble with her surfboard.

They came up to her. 'Can I give you a hand with that?' Scott nodded to the surfboard which was now threatening to slide out from her grasp altogether.

Her eyes were very blue against the bronze of her skin, and very clear. 'Yes, please,' she said with a smile of relief.

Scott eased the board out from beneath her arm, then tucking it under his own arm, held out his free hand. 'Hi. I'm Scott Robinson.'

She shook his hand, then looked expectantly at Mike. 'Oh, I'm Mike Young,' he said, also shaking hands with her.

'I'm Cassie Campbell,' she told them. 'For a moment there, I thought you two guys were brothers.'

Mike shook his head. 'No. Just two good mates,' he said.

'What do you guys do?' she asked.

'We're divers,' Mike told her with some pride.

'That's right,' Scott supplied. 'Double somersaults and all that type of stuff.'

'Oh, really?' Cassie looked impressed.

'Actually, we're in training.'

'Terrific.'

Mike gestured towards the surfboard Scott was holding under his arm. 'Do you know how to use this thing properly, or what?'

'I'm just learning,' Cassie said. 'But it keeps me fit.'

Very fit, Mike thought appreciatively as he gave her a quick sidelong glance. She looked as though she was almost bursting with good health.

They had reached the water's edge; the spent waves swirled foamily around their feet. Scott handed the board back to Cassie. 'There you go,' he said, giving it a tap.

'Thanks.'

They watched as she launched herself and the board into the waves. 'Very nice,' Mike observed.

'Sure is,' Scott agreed.

The board riders cut in obliquely across the white-capped walls of dark green water. Seagulls settled on the stone wall that separated the beach from the promenade above. Mike could feel the sun burning the salt into his body. This was the life, he thought drowsily.

'Hey, Mike,' Scott said suddenly. 'Isn't that Cassie?'

Mike sat up on his towel. Scott was on his feet, staring out past the line of breakers. Mike followed his gaze. He saw an empty board being swept in towards the shore. A short distance from it, he saw someone floundering clumsily in the water. He saw streaming yellow hair. He leapt up onto his feet. 'Yes, it is.'

'She looks as though she's in some sort of trouble.'

Mike began to sprint down the sand to the water. Scott ran after him. Mike ploughed through the water, then dived under the first wave as it thundered down on him. He dived under the next wave. He swam strongly towards Cassie.

'Are you all right?'

She was gasping. 'I – don't know. A cramp – .'

Reaching her, Mike lopped an arm around her waist, then began striking back towards the shore where some people were already staring curiously out at them. A wave rose beneath them and carried them forward for a short distance before rushing on ahead. Another wave loomed up behind them. Mike held the girl tightly in his arms as the breaking wave pounded down on them.

Then, feeling the sand beneath him, Mike struggled to his feet. He lifted the girl in his arms and carried her up on to the sand where Scott was waiting with her surfboard.

'She'll be okay,' Mike panted. 'She's got a cramp.'

'Put her down,' Scott commanded. 'Slowly.'

Cassie was moaning a little. Gently, Mike lowered her onto the sand. 'Are you okay?'

She was shivering. Water beaded her face, and her hair clung damply to her head. She snuggled closer to Mike as he continued to hold her in his arms. 'I think so.'

'Quite the hero, eh?' Scott said cheerfully as he patted Mike on the shoulder.

People were already beginning to gather around them. Realising this, and becoming a little embarrassed, Mike disengaged himself from Cassie. 'Do you think you can stand up?' he asked her.

She smiled faintly and nodded. He helped her on to her feet. She glanced around at the onlookers. 'Anyone would think they'd never seen a damsel in distress being rescued by a handsome knight before,' she remarked.

Scott laughed. 'Hey. I've heard him being called lots of things before,' he said, 'but never that.'

With the excitement now over, the spectators began to disperse. Cassie squeezed Mike's arm. 'That was almost a promising modelling career down the drain,' she said warmly. 'Thank you.'

Mike smiled shyly. 'I'm glad we were here.'

Scott had an idea. 'We're only just down the beach,' he said, pointing towards where they had left their towels and surfboards. 'If you want to join us . . . '

Cassie looked at Mike. 'Is that okay with you?'

'Sure.'

'Then I'll get my things,' she said, moving away from them.

They sat on the sand and watched the waves and the board riders. Farther out, sailing boats scudded down towards the Heads. Wisps of cloud drifted across the sky. When they decided they were hungry, Scott volunteered to fetch them something from the shop. 'Are you still at school?' Mike asked Cassie.

'I left after year ten,' she told him with a shake of her head.

'Then you really *are* a professional model?' Mike said in some awe.

'That's right.'

'Then I bet you get heaps of work.'

Cassie shrugged. 'I do all right.'

Scott returned with hamburgers and cans of soft drink. They ate and drank contentedly. 'I've got an idea,' Cassie said. 'Since you two guys are new around here, why don't I show you around a bit? Both of you, that is,' she added when Scott glanced uncertainly at Mike.

'Sounds okay to me,' Mike said.

'Okay then. When we leave we'll have a shower, get changed, then hit the town.'

'You're on,' Scott said enthusiastically. 'Do you live around here?'

'No. On the other side of town. I've got a flat.' Cassie looked at Mike. 'But you wouldn't mind if I had a shower at your place, would you?'

Mike was completely captivated by her. 'Ah, no. It's a really good shower.'

'It's great.' Scott confirmed.

'Terrific.' Cassie sipped her drink.

In the motel, she placed her bag down on the table and looked around the room that Mike shared with Scott. 'It's not too bad,' she pronounced.

Mike was doing his best to feel casual; although he certainly didn't feel it. 'It's not exactly home away from home,' he said airily, 'but it will do, I suppose.'

She smiled at him a little wickedly. 'Do for what?'

Mike became even more flustered. He tried to think for something suitably witty and worldly to say in reply. 'You can have the first shower if you like,' he said, gesturing towards the open bathroom door.

Scott had decided to remain on the beach for a while longer. He had winked at Mike behind Cassie's back. Cassie had been pleased: she had told Mike that they would now have more time to themselves, which, Mike had already suspected, was what she had really wanted all along. 'I don't suppose you're into conserving water?' she asked now from the bathroom door.

Mike stared at her, not believing that he had heard her correctly. Her smile was lazy and a little suggestive. 'You mean?'.

She chuckled softly and shook her head. 'Never mind.' She closed the bathroom door behind her.

She was under the shower for about ten minutes. When she finally emerged from the shower, she had only a towel wrapped around her. His pulse quickening, Mike stared at her. 'That was great,' she said. 'Nice and hot – the way I like it.'

'Ah . . . Can I get you something to drink?' he asked nervously. 'Orange juice or something?'

'Something stronger if you've got it.'

She was still wet. The towel barely covered her. 'I'm sorry,' Mike said. 'Our coach doesn't allow booze. It's too risky. I could make some coffee if you like.'

'I don't drink coffee. It's bad for you.'

She was making no attempt to get dressed. She was standing very close to him, covered only by the towel which barely reached the tops of her thighs. His lips were slightly parted; there was a seductive gleam in her eyes. Mike's pulse was racing by now; all his senses had quickened. 'I haven't thanked you yet for rescuing me,' she said rather huskily. 'I mean – properly.'

Suddenly, before Mike could realise what was happening, her arms were around him, her lips pressing hungrily against his. The towel loosened and fell gently on to the floor.

They met Cassie on the beach again the following morning. She had told Mike before leaving the motel room that she would see him there. He had been disappointed that she'd had to leave so soon; he had thought that they might be together for the rest of that day and evening. But no, she had told him she had to fly. She had an appointment, and would see him at the beach this morning. He had been looking out for her.

'I've been looking for you for hours,' she greeted him with a laugh. 'Well, ten minutes at least.' She kissed his ear.

It was still quite early, and there were not many people on the beach. They walked under the pines that lined the promenade. 'I've got my car,' she said after some moments. 'Do you want to come for a drive?'

'Well . . . '

'There's training, Mike,' Scott reminded him. 'We've got to keep working, mate.'

'But it's a beautiful day,' Cassie protested. 'You can't waste it.'

Mike demurred. 'The diving competition is pretty important.'

Cassie regarded him coquettishly. 'More important than having fun?'

'Well, I don't know . . . '

'Better not, Mike,' Scott warned.

Mike thought about it some more. He really did want to be with Cassie. He was totally smitten. 'Once won't hurt, will it?' he queried.

'You can come too, Scott,' Cassie offered brightly. 'If you wish.'

'No thanks.' Scott turned to Mike. 'I could cover for you, I suppose.'

Mike clapped him joyfully on the shoulder. 'Thanks, mate,' he said with a broad grin.

They drove away from the breach, heading west in Cassie's small Japanese car. She drove fast and surely. She told Mike that she had to go back to her flat first; there was a little job she had to do, which wouldn't take long. After that they would have the rest of the day to themselves.

About three-quarters of an hour later, Cassie pulled up outside an apartment block that looked reasonably new. 'Here we are,' she announced. 'My humble home.' She glanced at her watch. 'Oh dear, I'm late.'

There was someone already inside her flat, a youngish man with rather wild hair. Seeing him, and for a moment believing that he lived with Cassie, Mike experienced a twinge of jealousy. Cassie had said nothing to him about living with anyone. 'Mike, this is Roger Yates,' Cassie informed him. 'Roger's a stunning photographer. He's got his own key,' she explained, 'so he can let himself in and set up everything.'

It was then that Mike noticed the photographic equipment in the living room. He saw the camera on its tripod, the lights that had been set up, the boxes of film. He shook hands with the photographer.

'Okay,' Roger said to Cassie. 'Are you nearly ready?'

'Give me a couple of minutes.' Cassie disappeared into the bedroom.

Quite bewildered by what was happening, Mike sat awkwardly on the edge of a chair while Roger made adjustments to his camera equipment and took light readings. Mike looked around the room, which, he saw, was quite nicely furnished. There was a television set, sound equipment, a book case, pictures on the walls and a few pot plants. Then

Cassie, draped in a dressing gown, returned to the living room.

'Ready now?' Roger asked her.

'I'm ready.'

With a quick smile at Mike, Cassie slowly took off her dressing gown. To Mike's complete astonishment, she was wearing nothing beneath it.

Shock turned to embarrassment, then smouldering resentment as Cassie, quite unselfconsciously and with perfect assurance, posed for picture after picture. 'Okay,' Roger said at last, 'I think we can call it a day. You can get dressed now.'

Cassie pulled on her dressing gown. 'I won't be a minute, Mike,' she said, heading for the bedroom.

Still angry and embarrassed by what he had just witnessed, Mike stood up and moved across to Roger who was beginning to dismantle his equipment. Roger glanced up at him shrewdly; he must have been aware of Mike's disapproval. 'I take it you didn't know what sort of modelling Cassie was involved in,' he said.

'I didn't know she had to take her clothes off,' Mike said tautly. 'No.'

'And you think I belong under a rock,' Roger said matter-of-factly.

'It's your business, I suppose,' Mike observed coldly. 'I still think there are better ways to make a living.'

'Do you now?' Roger was studying him with obvious interest. 'Look,' he went on after a brief pause, 'I used to do industrial photography. Do you know what that is?'

'Well . . .

'You take photographs of factories,' Roger continued without waiting for an answer, 'mining sheds, pieces of equipment.' He smiled ironically. 'A real art form. Anyway, I thought it was about time for me to move on. I didn't see myself getting anywhere with pulleys and conveyor belts – so I got myself a job with one of the more upmarket magazines. There I found myself photographing pieces of crockery, and lounge suites, and French salads. So, boyo, I told myself, it's time to proceed to even greater challenges.'

'Like this?' Mike gestured towards the couch where Cassie had done most of her posing.

Roger was still regarding him thoughtfully. 'No, you don't approve, do you? Look,' he went on more earnestly. 'The human body is the most marvellous creation. It's beautiful. Given the right lighting, the right mood . . . the textures and shapes can be magnificent.'

For anyone else perhaps, Mike thought sourly, but this was Cassie he was talking about. After what had happened between them yesterday . . . He shook his head. No, he wasn't convinced: he didn't think it was right, despite textures and shapes and lighting, and all the rest of it, to pose nude for photographs that would end up God only knew where. 'Who buys them?' he asked.

'If we're lucky we might make a sale to a magazine.' Roger smiled ruefully. 'Most of the time we're not lucky.'

'Then if you *do* make a sale? I mean, what sort of people get to see them?'

'People who can appreciate them,' Roger answered. 'They'll see a good model working hard at her craft – and believe me, Cassie *is* very good at what she does.'

Mike was sorry he had come. His eyes had been opened for him in a way he had least expected. He didn't like what Cassie was doing and he didn't like the possessive way in which this guy talked about her. The day had suddenly turned sour for him – and what was more, he had wasted precious time when he should have been training. He decided that there was no point in waiting for Cassie to return fully dressed again from the bedroom. With a curt nod to the photographer, he moved across to the hall door and let himself out.

He was still bitter the following morning when Cassie met him on the path running beneath the cliffs that enclosed the southern end of the beach. He had been walking and thinking, and staring at the waves as they swirled over and between the slippery weed-covered rocks below him. He could feel the spray on his face, taste the salt on his lips. The day was overcast and there were not many people on the beach.

'Hello, Mike.'

He turned and looked at her with a closed expression. He hadn't expected to see her again. Her fair hair had been tousled by the breeze which was gradually strengthening. She was smiling at him a little tentatively. 'Oh, hi.'

'You disappeared so suddenly yesterday.'

'Yeah, I'm sorry.' Mike knew he could have handled it better than he had. He had owed her an explanation at least. 'I just wanted to get out.'

Moving across the low stone wall that bordered the path, he sat down on it. Cassie sat down next to him. 'Roger said you were upset, but at least you could have told me you were going.'

Mike nodded unhappily. 'I know. But I just couldn't help it.' He was staring out to sea, but was conscious of the fact that she was staring at him.

'I thought you liked me,' she said after a longish pause.

That was the trouble – that was the whole trouble. He saw her as he had seen her the previous day, naked and posing under the photographer's lights, changing position at his instruction – and he saw her, too, as many others would see her, if Roger was luckier in selling his pictures than he had been most times before. 'I do like you,' he said miserably. 'Very much. 'But yesterday – It wasn't what I expected.'

'Taking my clothes off, you mean?'

'Well, yes, to be honest.'

'It's a job,' she said. 'It's nothing more than that. I'm proud of my body, if you must know, and I don't see anything wrong. Anyway, Roger says I'm one of the best models he has.'

Roger again – it was always Roger. Roger says this, Roger says that. Mike grunted. 'I'll bet he does.'

'He's a professional photographer,' Cassie said patiently. 'He's my friend, and I trust him.'

'Obviously.'

And just as obviously, Cassie's patience with him had been exhausted. She pushed herself up from the wall. 'Oh, you can think what you like,' she exclaimed. 'It's *my* body, and I'll do what I like with it.'

Mike looked up at her. 'Oh sure,' he said harshly. 'What do *you* care? As long as you get paid for it.'

She slapped him across the face, hard. Mike rocked on the stone wall. 'I'm independent,' she cried. 'I thought you would understand that. You've got no right to criticise me for what I do – and at least *I* don't judge people.'

She was plainly very upset. Swinging abruptly away from him, she began to head back down the path with quick, agitated steps. His face still stinging from where she had struck him, Mike sprang to his feet. 'Cassie, look . . . '

She stopped and turned back to face him. Her eyes were like chips of ice; her lips were taut so that she virtually had to spit out her parting words to him. 'I'm sorry I ever met you,' she said with unmistakable finality, then turning once more on her heel, continued to walk hurriedly down the path towards the beach.

Mike stared unhappily after her. He knew it was no use following her, catching up with her and trying to explain to her how he felt at this very moment. He had already had his chance – and he had just gone and blown it.

Four

Married at last – at long last. A miracle had been wrought. Des still couldn't believe it. 'You may kiss me now,' Daphne had said, clutching her bouquet.

'I know,' Des had said with a sheepish smile while everyone looked on with beams of approval – and perhaps relief. 'It's been a long wait.'

Deep down, no one – Des probably more than anyone else – had believed it would happen. Surely the bad luck that had dogged him in the past would once more reassert itself at the last minute. But no, this time it had all been carried off with the utmost smoothness. There had been no standing around at the altar in a cold sweat while the clergyman kept glancing at his wristwatch and the congregation shifted uneasily in their pews; there had been no sinking feeling that came with the realisation that once again he had been left in the lurch. Four times it had happened before; it was a sensation with which he had become familiar. He gazed fondly at his new wife. Was it really true? Was it just a dream from which he was about to be brutally awakened?

He had stood there in something of a daze as the clergyman intoned those magic words at the nuptial hitching post. He was the same clergyman who had kept glancing at his watch on those earlier occasions – his eyes had instinctively and in resignation turned heavenward when Des had approached him, fingers crossed, for what he hoped fervently would be for the last time. As he listened to the man speak of that lifelong union in which man and woman were called so to give themselves in body, mind and spirit, Des had been mentally braced for the hurricane that would undoubtedly blow in on them and, lifting the roof of the church, send it spinning off into the turbulence that was already filled with flying objects. But . . . no hurricane. The clergyman had referred to the joys and sorrows of life, and Des, fingers still crossed along the seam of the trousers of his best suit, had waited for the semi-trailer, out of control, to burst in through the stone wall of the church. 'In prosperity and adversity . . . ' Masked bandits? One of the older members of the congregation struck down by a heart attack? A fainting fit? So far, so good . . . ' Faithfulness and strength.' Ah . . .

'If any person here can show why Des and Daphne may not be lawfully joined in marriage, he should speak now or hereafter remain in silence.' Des had held his breath. An old boyfriend, an ex-husband he hadn't known about . . . The silence had been overpowering and larded with the sweet aroma of a variety of flowers. No objection, no dramatic scene.

The ceremony had continued, and there had been no fire or pestilence to send everyone scattering, no bomb scares, nor tidal waves, nor earthquakes, nor stampeding buffalo. Everything going to plan – so far.

'. . . Take you, Daphne Rose, to be my lawfully wedded wife . . .'

No axe-wielding madman; no hordes of killer wasps.

'. . . and to hold from this day forward . . .'

No landslides nor summonses for tax evasion.

'. . . for better or for worse . . .'

No shipwrecks nor train derailments.

And so it had gone on, the ritual pronounced and repeated – and nothing had happened! Des's fingers had remained crossed throughout; he had held his breath and expected disaster.

'. . . God hath joined together, let no man put asunder . . .'

If anything was to happen, if the cataclysm was to descend on their slightly bowed heads, it would be now. Des had been sweating quite freely by then. And then . . . 'In the name of God, I declare them to be husband and wife.'

Done. They had sailed through it without catastrophe. There had seemed to be a general exhalation of breath throughout the church. Married at last. 'You may kiss the bride,' the clergyman had invited.

'You may kiss me now,' Daphne had said, her eyes shining as she turned her face up to his.

'I know,' Des had said just before he kissed her. 'It's been a long wait.'

That was the marriage ceremony over: there was still the reception, and then the honeymoon to come.

At last, they were alone. The reception had passed without mishap. A few people got drunk, and Clive Gibbons, who had given the bride away, had read the telegrams. There had been a lot of hand-shaking, a lot of kissing, and a furtive tear or two. Daphne had been radiant. And finally they had got away.

The guest house stood on the side of a mountain and looked out over other mountains that stretched away to the horizon. Trees grew to fantastic heights, and crystal clear streams trickled down over rocky beds. There were paths to walk, and few signs of other people. Des had chosen the place before his previous vigil in front of the altar. On that occasion already half convinced that the worst was about to happen, he had taken Daphne's late arrival as confirmation of this and had fled the church only moments before Daphne finally did arrive. He learnt that later – but by that time, of course, Desmond had contracted a severe case of cold feet from which it took him some months to recover.

But that was then; now was now – and he was a married man on his honeymoon. On the first night, he ordered champagne, and placed a red rose on Daphne's pillow while she was in the bathroom. Later, forgetting that the rose was there, he pricked his arm on a thorn as he gently laid his bride down on the bed. In the morning, there were petals scattered over the bedclothes.

Des was the first to awake. Rolling over in the bed, he kissed Daphne on the neck and then on the shoulder. 'Good morning,' he said as she stirred.

'Is it?' she mumbled sleepily. 'Already?'

'I'm afraid so.'

She yawned and stretched, and turned over on to her back. 'I don't want to get up.'

It had been long after midnight last night when he switched off the light, and it had been a long day before that. Now the sun was streaming in through the window of the room in which they had spent their first night as husband and wife. This was to be their room for two delicious weeks to come. 'You don't have to get up,' he whispered in her ear. 'We're on our honeymoon – remember?'

'Oh yes.' Daphne smiled drowsily. 'I remember.'

'And, anyway, we've ordered breakfast in bed.'

'I could easily get used to that.'

Des began to kiss her with increasing passion. 'I just can't believe we're here.' At long last, after many fits and starts, back-pedallings and heartache, they were here at last.

Daphne placed her finger on the tip of his nose. 'You'd better believe it. Man and wife. Till death do us part.' Withdrawing her finger, she studied the ring which Des had slipped on her wedding finger the previous afternoon. 'It took me long enough to get that on,' she said reflectively. 'And I'm not taking it off – not now or never.'

Des kissed the ring. 'Suits me.'

Breakfast arrived. Des brought the tray across to the bed. 'Is that all we get?' Daphne asked. 'Toast and marmalade? And tea?'

Des placed the tray down on the bedside table. 'What more do you want?'

'Oh, bacon and eggs at least.' She gave him a slow, sleepy smile. 'Being married makes me hungry.'

'Ah, yes.'

Des kissed her fiercely. Her hands clasped around his neck, Daphne brought him down on to the bed. Breakfast could wait for the time being.

Afterwards, they went for a walk along one of the mountain paths. There was still a chill in the early morning air and the contours of the distant mountains were softened by a slight haze. It promised to be another flawless day. They walked hand in hand along the path as moisture dripped from the leaves of the trees that towered above them. They were happy; Des was feeling quite light-headed. And passionate. These early days of his much-delayed marriage would be ruled by their undiluted passion. This much understood, they hurried back to their room – and that was where, lurking in the wings all this time, waiting for a chance to pounce at a time when it would be least suspected, disaster finally caught up with them.

The wedding had gone without a hitch, and the reception afterwards had been no more rowdy than was to be expected – but now, on their honeymoon, in their room that overlooked the distant hazy mountains, Des, in a burst of exuberance, decided to indulge in some horseplay. He decided to play the caveman.

With a deep growling sound, he had just scooped Daphne up off her feet and was carrying her across to the bed while she squealed with delight and called him a brute. Still making his strange guttural noises, he threw her down onto the bed – and there was a loud and ominous clicking sound, a stab of fierce pain. 'Oh no,' he groaned, clutching the lower part of his back where the agony was building up.

Daphne stopped bouncing on the bed. 'Des, what's wrong?'

'It's my back,' Des gasped. 'I think I've put it out.'

The agony was very real. He couldn't straighten; he couldn't do anything. Still clutching his back, he groaned and hobbled. 'There are more subtle ways of telling your wife to go on a diet, you know,' Daphne said in mild rebuke. Then, as Des tried to lower himself onto the bed, as he grunted and groaned, she was suddenly alerted to the fact that the matter was more serious than she had thought. 'Des?'

'Just help me get on to the – bed.'

The pain was ferocious; there had never been so much pain concentrated in the one area. When Daphne took his arm to help him, he almost screamed with pain. But in the end, they managed it. With Daphne guiding him, Des gingerly eased himself down on to the bed.

'It could be just a cramp,' Daphne suggested. 'Some massage would possibly do the trick.'

Des was lying face down on the bed. He knew only too well what had happened. It would take more than massage to get rid of the pain. 'It . . . it's a slipped disc, Daph.'

'What?'

'I've had one before.'

'Oh, Des.'

She didn't have to say it: he knew what she was thinking. The first full day of their honeymoon, and *this* had to happen – just because he had taken it into his head to do some clowning. 'I know,' he muttered irritably. 'I know.'

Daphne sighed. 'I suppose I had better get you a doctor.'

'I've ruined everything,' Des said miserably.

Daphne tried to sound reassuring. 'Don't worry, Tarzan. Our life will be one long continual honeymoon.' She bent over to kiss him; there was another vicious stab of pain, and Des yelped. Daphne straightened. 'Let's cut out the caveman stuff in future, shall we?' she said unnecessarily.

'It's sore, Daphne,' Des said with another groan.

Daphne found a doctor who examined Des, who prodded him here and there and asked if it hurt. When Des finally screamed, he seemed quite satisfied.

'How did it happen?' he asked.

There was an embarrassed silence. 'I was – ah – I was lifting something,' Des said at last.

'Oh? What were you lifting?'

Des and Daphne answered at the same time. Des said, 'Chair', and Daphne said, 'Suitcase.' Des hastily tried to retrieve the situation. 'The suitcase was on the chair,' he said.

But this doctor was a knowing man: he was no novice to such complaints. 'How long have you folks been married?' he asked.

'Since yesterday,' Daphne replied glumly.

The doctor chuckled. 'Honeymooner's back.'

'What?'

'It's an old injury,' Des muttered unconvincingly.

'Look, son.' The medical man regarded Des with sympathy. 'We get a lot of honeymooners up here, and dislocated backs account for more than half my business. And I've heard every excuse, believe you me. One of these days, when I retire, I'm going to put some of them in a book.' He began to write on a referral pad he had taken from his bag. 'I'll arrange to have you admitted to the local hospital here for a few days.'

'What?' Des was dismayed.

'No, Doctor,' Daphne pleaded. 'Please . . .'

The doctor stopped writing on his pad. He looked thoughtfully up at Daphne. 'Well the only alternative is for you to drive him home,' he said, 'but taking it *very* slowly. No more than one hour at a time. And then get onto your local doctor and arrange a physiotherapist.' He replaced the pad in his bag which he then closed. 'It will do you no good, hanging around here.'

Daphne walked with him to the door. 'Thanks, Doctor.'

'Let me know what you decide.' He turned back to Des. 'Oh, and in future, young man, do like the Romans, and make haste slowly. You'll live longer.'

Daphne closed the door behind him, then returned to the bed where her husband of less than twenty-four hours was feeling no better. She looked down at him enquiringly. 'Shall we leave?'

'Sorry, Daph.' Des was feeling totally abject.

Gently, she patted his leg. 'I'll start packing.' She was about halfway across the room when she stopped and laughed. 'You know something, Des?' She pointed. 'The suitcase *was* on the chair.'

Des would have laughed right along with her if it hadn't hurt so much.

Five

Clive hadn't meant to come out with it like that. It had always been something personal and very private with him, and it was still a part of him, an old wound that would never heal properly. But his brother had become so insistent about it. He just couldn't understand what had gotten into Clive, he nagged, throwing away his talent like that, playing the fool, and being the total idiot around the place. Why hadn't he followed up a career after such a promising start, instead of chucking it in just so he could do crazy things like delivering gorillagrams and whatever other hare–brained notion entered his head. But–and this was something Graham was unable to understand, he being the strait–laced member of the family – Clive enjoyed doing these things; he thrived on challenges. He didn't want wealth or fame. He just wanted to do his own thing. But Graham had continued to niggle at him.

'Didn't your medical training have any effect on you at all?'

'Sure.' Clive had shrugged offhandedly. 'A negative one.'

'For heaven's sake.' Graham had shown his exasperation with the feckless younger brother who was throwing away all his chances. 'You're wasting your talent. It was always an uphill slog for me. I had to struggle for everything I got.'

That was all right for Graham. He was well-suited for the medical life with its disciplines and life–and–death decisions. 'I've heard all this before,' Clive had reminded him wearily.

'Then you obviously need to hear it again.'

Finally, Clive had given up. 'You just can't leave me alone, can you?' he had almost shouted. 'You have to keep pushing it. All right, then, if you *really* want to know why I gave up medicine – the real reason I gave it up – okay, I'll tell you.'

And he had begun to tell his brother the real reason why he had given up medicine. He told his brother about Linda. 'She was beautiful, and funny, and intelligent.' She was also dead. 'We were going to get married,' he said. The bitter memories were returning as he spoke. 'She died of cerebral haemorrhage one night while I was rostered on Casualty. She was at home. I was at work with drunks and street kids. She had rung me that night, earlier, to tell me that she had a blinding headache and to ask what should she do about it. I had snapped at her. A headache wasn't something to get all hot and bothered about, I said. I told her to take two aspirins and go to bed.'

'I think I'm beginning to understand,' Graham said quietly.

'Are you?' Clive looked up sharply at his brother, then shook his head. 'She never rang me at work before,' he said. 'I'd never known her to have a headache. But I put work first.'

'That's because you had to do that. Your first responsibility was to your patients.'

That was Graham's attitude. It wasn't Clive's. 'Your first responsibility is to the people you love.'

'Yes and no,' Graham said thoughtfully. 'It's not so clear–cut as that. As a doctor . . . '

'I'm *not* a doctor, Graham,' Clive interrupted. 'It's time you came to terms with that.'

'No, I mean it, Clive. It was tragic, I know, but it wasn't your fault. You *must* be able to see that.'

Graham was rationalising, which Clive was simply not able to do. He blamed himself as he was sure Graham would blame *himself* if something similar had happened to Katie, his wife, or little Vicki. It was quite easy for Graham to be calm and rational about it from the sidelines.

'I wish you'd come to me,' Graham went on after an uncomfortable silence. 'I might have been able to help you through it.'

Nobody could have helped him through it. 'It was something I had to do for myself,' Clive said quietly.

Graham regarded him severely over the top of his spectacles. 'And you were prepared to let us think you were just copping out, that you couldn't hack any more.'

Clive shrugged. 'It seemed the easiest way of dealing with it,' he said with a rueful smile. 'But there you go. The truth's out now.'

Yes, the truth was out now – and it triggered off something quite remarkable. It brought Linda back from the dead.

When he answered the door that evening a couple of weeks later, and saw Linda standing there, he was stunned. He stared at her in amazement. 'Hi,' she said awkwardly. 'I'm Louise Lawry. Linda's sister.'

Yes, he could see now that it wasn't Linda. But the likeness was extraordinary. She had Linda's eyes, and her hair. 'This is a surprise.'

'I suppose it must be.' They shook hands. 'I hope this isn't inconvenient,' Linda's sister said. 'I felt a little funny, calling on a complete stranger.'

'Not at all.' Clive stood to one side. 'Come in.'

He was flustered. He felt awkward. He ushered her into the living room. Yes, even Linda's walk. 'Linda and I were very alike,' she remarked with a nervous laugh.

'Alike?' Clive was still taken aback by the resemblance. 'You're a double.' Linda had told him about her sister, but he hadn't met her; she had been overseas at the time. 'You could be twins.'

'Actually Linda was two years older than me.'

'Yeah . . . Look, sit down, why don't you?' Clive gestured towards a chair. 'Can I get you a drink, or something?'

'Coffee would be nice.'

'Fine.'

Clive made coffee. 'I was overseas when she was sick,' Louise said later. 'I've only just arrived back, in fact. I . . . couldn't get here for the funeral . . . and . . . well, afterwards, there didn't really seem to be much point.'

'I guess not.' Clive nodded understandingly and

sipped his coffee. He had more or less recovered from his shock by now.

'She wrote to me about you,' Louise continued. 'That's why I wanted to come and see you. I felt I owed it to you.'

'I'm glad you did.'

'She told me a lot about you. In her letters. They were full of this exciting Doctor Clive Gibbons she had met.'

'Yes,' Clive said sadly. 'We had quite a good thing going there for a while.'

'I'm sorry.'

'No, I'm the one who should be sorry. I should have done more. I should have realised.'

'You shouldn't blame yourself.' Then, as she studied him, something occurred to her. 'That's not why you gave up medicine, is it?'

'Partly.'

'But that's crazy.'

'Maybe I just needed some time to get over it,' Clive said unhappily, then realising he was becoming maudlin, shook himself out of it. 'Oh, enough of this,' he said more brightly, then had an idea. 'Say, what are you doing for dinner tonight?'

'I've made no plans.'

'Because I know a great little place not far from here.'

'Lassiter's?'

'You know it?'

'I'm staying there.'

Clive stood up. 'I'll get my jacket.'

'Fine,' Louise said with a smile.

They had dinner at Lassiter's. They had oysters and veal and a bottle of excellent Chardonnay. They talked and joked. They discussed their hopes and aspirations.

'I've really enjoyed myself,' Louise said over coffee.

'Me too. It was just like . . . ' Clive stopped himself. He had been about to say 'old times'. Old times with Linda. He changed the subject. 'Listen, while you're in Erinsborough, will you be doing the tourist circuit?'

She looked momentarily confused. 'Sorry?'

'Sightseeing.'

'Are you kidding? This is Erinsborough. With a capital 'E' for entertainment.'

Now she was looking amused. 'Such as?'

Such as . . . 'I'll take you. A personally conducted tour. Your feet won't touch the floor, you'll thrill to the spectacle, you'll be amazed by the . . . '

'Don't oversell it, Clive. Of course, I'd love to.'

' . . . age-old charm, the people, the hist . . . You'd love to?'

'That's what I said.'

'Wonderful,' Clive said happily. 'A treat in store. An experience that will be truly memorable.'

He picked Louise up quite early the following morning from the hotel. She was wearing slacks and sensible shoes. They set out on their tour of discovery. 'Here we have a fine example of neo–poverty architecture,' he said, pointing to a dilapidated row of terrace houses.

'Neo–what?'

'Terrace houses,' he told her. 'Built for the working–class man, bought out by the trendies, and destined for millionaires.'

Louise laughed. She was enjoying herself hugely. 'Oh, Clive. You can't keep this up.'

Clive was forging ahead again. 'Next on our itinerary is a rare treat. A place of great historical significance. As crammed with culture as an art gallery or a museum. One day it will be an archaeological site.'

'Where are you taking me?'

'The Council rubbish tip.'

Louise began to laugh. Clive sobered. 'That's just the way she used to laugh,' he said quietly.

Louise stopped laughing. 'Clive,' she said seriously. 'I'm not Linda.'

'I know, I know.' Clive brightened again. 'So how are you enjoying the tour so far?'

'It's great,' Louise said cheerfully. 'You should do it professionally. You'd make a small fortune.'

'Hey, that's not a bad idea.'

They continued their tour, and under Clive's expert and enthusiastic guidance, Louise came to know the stately edifice of the local gasometer, the exciting brick façade of the Council chambers, the grand sweep of the park that had a small lake in the middle of it, the school and the fire station. By this time, they were almost back at Ramsay Street. 'How about a cup of coffee before we go on with the tour?' Clive suggested.

'You mean there's more to see?'

'We've only just started. Why? Have you had enough?'

'I'm in your hands.'

'Ah–ha.'

'So what's next on the itinerary?' Louise asked.

Clive thought for a moment. 'Well, there's the sewage plant.'

Louise wrinkled her nose. 'Oh yuk.'

'Or there's the railway station. Very educational.'

'How come?'

'Best graffiti around these parts. Very high standard.'

'Well, where do *you* want to go?'

'I don't mind,' Clive replied with a smile. 'I'm happy whatever we do.'

They had coffee at the house, then, deciding to take a picnic lunch with them on the next stage of their tour of Erinsborough and its attractions, they set about preparing it. 'Are you sure you feel up to a full day on the move?' Clive asked as he sliced the corned beef.

Louise was buttering the bread. 'Hah, are you kidding? These feet have walked all over Europe. And hurry up with that corned beef, ape man.'

'Ape man?'

'Sorry. I couldn't resist.'

Clive was aware of her closeness. 'I'm very sensitive,' he said, placing the knife on the cutting board'

'And slow off the mark. Or don't you want any meat on these sandwiches?'

'Boy, you know how to crack the whip, don't you?' Clive remarked.

'Yes, and I'm looking forward to this picnic.' She looked up at him. 'Where will we be having it? Have you got any ideas?'

Clive had a splendid idea. 'On a desert island.'

'Where on earth do you find a desert island around here?'

'Actually, it's more of a traffic island,' he told her. 'But it's very deserted because most people can't run fast enough to dodge the cars.'

Louise rolled her eyes up towards the ceiling. 'What am I letting myself in for?' she groaned.

'Fun.' Clive picked up a salami from the counter. 'Here, catch.' He tossed it to her. She missed it and it fell on to the floor. They both bent to pick it up, and almost collided. They looked into each other's eyes. They were very close.

'I hope the floor's clean,' Louise remarked.

'Why would an ex–doctor have a dirty floor?'

'Oh, Linda used to say that they were the . . . ' Louise stopped. 'Sorry. I didn't mean . . . '

'It's all right,' Clive said. 'I don't mind talking about her.'

'That's good.'

There was a brief but strained silence as they continued with their preparations for a picnic on a traffic island. Clive picked up a bottle of tomato sauce and began to shake it over a sandwich he was making. A dark red glob splashed onto the map of the district which was open on the counter in front of him. 'Oh, damn, look at that.'

'What?' She came up behind him to peer over his shoulder.

Clive pointed. 'Right on our picnic spot, here.'

Louise laughed in much the way Linda would have laughed. Clive turned, and she was standing so close to him that their lips almost met. It was a moment fraught with possibilities. Then, nervously, aware of the vibrance that suddenly existed between them, Louise backed away and returned to making her sandwiches, all the while chattering in a rather forced manner. 'In Europe you often see people on the median strip . . . anywhere where there's some grass.' Clive continued to stare at her. She was avoiding his eye. 'Did you want mustard on these sandwiches?' she asked.

'Just stop for a minute,' Clive said quietly.

She still wasn't looking at him. 'We've got to get this show on the road.'

'Hey.' He moved across to her, then placing his hands on her shoulders, he eased her around to face him. She didn't resist him until he was just about to kiss her.

'Don't.'

'Why not?'

'Well, it's . . . ' She sighed and shook her head.

'Is it because of Linda?'

'No, it's not that.'

He was still holding her by the shoulders. 'Is it me? A ratbag? A no–hoper? Too good–looking for you? I'll change.'

'I'm engaged.'

He released her. 'What? Why didn't you tell me?'

'I thought it would remind you too much of Linda,' she said softly. 'I mean, you would have been married by now, if . . . Well, you know. I felt it would hurt you too much if I talked about Nick and me.'

'Nick? Who's Nick?'

'He's a social worker. In London. We're going to be married as soon as I get back.'

Clive tried to hide his disappointment by adopting an air of flippancy. 'Don't get the wrong idea,' he said lightly. 'It's just that I never miss a chance to kiss a beautiful girl.'

'Oh . . . ' Louise smiled a little shakily.

'So it's on with the picnic?' Clive asked.

'I don't know. I don't think so.' She shook her head again. 'I think I'd better go.'

'You don't have to.'

'I think I'd better.' She gave him a sisterly kiss on the cheek. 'I'm sorry.'

Clive, still trying to make a joke of it, tapped the region near his heart with his forefinger. 'Cast iron,' he said bravely.

Then, as Louise left the house, his smile faded. He had missed out again. That was too bad – it was terrible. He was suddenly very depressed.

But she had given him an idea during their walking tour of Erinsborough's places of interest. Now, to take his mind off the disappointment, he began to work on with a will. Walking tours of the district were a great idea:There was money to be made, and fame to be spread far and wide. But he needed a name. 'Terrific Trips'? 'Weird Walks'? 'Wacky Tours'? 'Tacky Tours'? What was better. He made notes and studied them. 'Forget the tourist traps,' he wrote on his foolscap pad. 'Try Tacky Tours. See the city from the underside. From the graffiti in the public loos to the garbage bins of the rich. All the secrets of the city laid bare.' He liked it very much.

But it still didn't stop him from thinking about Louise, whom he had mistaken for Linda when she had turned up on the doorstep that evening. They'd had fun together, and Louise had laughed in just the way Linda had laughed when she was alive. And then, for Clive, things had become serious – and Louise had told him she was engaged to someone called Nick who was a social worker in London. With a wistful sigh, Clive underlined the words 'Tacky Tours' at the top of his foolscap pad.

Des and Daphne Clarke were on their honeymoon. Clive had agreed to look after Daphne's coffee shop while they were away. On that particular morning, he was just checking out the float in the till when the door opened and in walked Louise. He was surprised. It had been more than a week since he had last seen her. He gestured towards one of the tables. 'Take a seat. Do you want a cup of coffee?'

'Take it easy,' she said. 'The coffee's not so important,'

'So how are you?' he asked.

'Not too well.'

'Oh?'

'Been missing a friend,' she explained. 'You haven't been in touch.'

'I'm a busy man,' he told her. 'Besides, I thought you might have flown back to London. You know, your fiancé.' He was sounding quite casual about it, underplaying his feelings altogether.

Her eyes flickered momentarily away from his. 'It doesn't mean we can't be friends, does it?'

'Of course not. Look,' he said. 'We still haven't had that picnic on the median strip I promised you.'

'But you're working today.'

'I'll get Mrs Clarke to take over. We can still go on our guided tour. That's if you're still interested.'

'I thought it was just a joke,' Louise said, smiling. 'The median strip. I mean.'

'No joke,' he assured her. 'We'll have a great time. I once knew a guy who lived on a median strip. He said it was a fantastic place to live – good lighting, good amenities, good drainage. The only problem was in leaving it. He said you had to be doing at least sixty miles an hour.'

Louise laughed, and again it was a true echo of Linda that brought with it a very real pang for Clive.

Later, as they stood beside the stormwater canal that ran behind Lassiter's Hotel, Clive expounded his idea of Tacky Tours. 'As concepts go,' he said, 'I'd say it could be big.'

'Definitely,' Louise said.

'I mean, the world is full of tacky places.'

'Absolutely.'

'The Americans would love it.'

'You could try Europe.'

'Yes, and England.' Clive sighed. He meant to mention England, where Louise's fiancé was a social worker, helping the poor and needy and generally performing good works. He gestured impatiently. 'Okay, we don't talk about England, or your fiancé. Friends we are, and friends we're going to stay – right?'

'Right.'

'So what's next on the agenda?' Looking around him, Clive's lighted on the car park of the Lassiter Hotel complex. 'Ah yes, the incredible scenic magnificence of the car park,' he said in tones of awe.

They stopped to have a drink in the Waterhole Bar of the hotel. There was a darts game in progress. 'And here we have another item of local interest,' Clive intoned. 'The ancient and noble art of archery in its proletarian form. Note the intense concentration.'

The dart players glared at him. Clive ordered a light beer for himself and a gin and tonic for Louise, then brought them back to the table. He told her about his career as an opal miner in Lightning Ridge and about the kangaroo that acted as the local postman. 'I don't believe you,' Louise said.

'As I live and breathe.' Suddenly, Clive clutched his chest and slumped in the chair. There was a cheer from the dartboard. One of the players had just landed the bull. Clive straightened in his chair and grinned at Louise.

'You're weird,' she said.

'Thank you.'

Then Louise became serious. 'Clive, I've got a confession to make.'

'Oh, and what's that?'

Louise hesitated. She looked down at her drink thoughtfully, then back up at him. 'Well, let's just say that you're not the only one around here who has been spinning yarns,' she said at last. 'My fiancé in London . . . Nick . . . '

Nick the social worker, the tireless benefactor of humanity. Clive's face fell. 'Oh yes?' he said warily.

'He's an ex–fiancé.'

What words these were for him to hear! Nick would have to do his good works alone! Clive tried to play down his delight. 'You broke up?'

Louise nodded. 'Two months ago.'

Confusion was now replacing Clive's initial joy. 'I don't get it,' he said with a puzzled frown. 'Why lie?'

There was another hesitation. 'Because, Clive Gibbons, if you haven't noticed it by now, you probably never will. Well, let's say . . . Oh, I don't know it's not easy.' Louise smiled nervously, and stared down at her glass again. 'Well, I am rather attracted to you,' she said with an obvious effort.

Clive could have cheered as the dart players had just cheered. He could have performed a hand–spring or danced around the room. Instead, he said, 'And you lied because?'

'Because everything was going so fast.'

'And now?'

She placed her hand on his own. 'Why don't you stop asking questions and . . . kiss me.'

Clive didn't need to be asked a second time. Raising himself from his chair, he reached across the table and kissed her on the lips. The dart players cheered again.

They kissed again, and more fully, when they returned to Clive's house and were sitting side by side on the sofa. But suddenly Clive pulled away from her.

Louise looked at him in dismay. 'You don't want this?'

'I love this, I crave this,' Clive assured her. 'It's just that I'm a bit nervous.'

'Oh . . . ' Louise smiled in relief. 'Like I was?'

'Romance and I don't exactly have the best track record,' Clive said ruefully.

'Meaning?'

'Meaning, how about we take this one day at a time? Let me get used to the idea.'

'Yes. That might help me, too.'

'Terrific.' Clive beamed at her.

'One day at a time,' Louise said.

'Who knows?' Clive said brightly. 'Maybe we can string enough days together to make a week.'

'Maybe even a month.'

'I like it.'

'Me, too.'

They kissed again. It was a long lingering kiss. Clive was ecstatic. It looked as though his run of bad luck as far as the opposite sex was concerned had just come to an end.

There was some more Tacky Touring to complete – the possibilities of the district had by no means been exhausted. There was the Returned Servicemen's Club to admire, the statue of Queen Victoria opposite the courthouse and the two Chinese restaurants. There was the taxi rank and the new roundabout, the newsagents and the chemist's shop on the corner. There were the other shops that catered to all the needs of the vibrant and cosmopolitan community of Erinsborough. And then, of course, there was Clive's fascinating new market survey to keep them occupied. They had counted cats.

It was a fact, Clive had learned, that in that fair suburb there was a three to one ratio in favour of black cats as opposed to tabbies, Siamese, Burmese and sundry feline strays. It was already dark before they had time to start on the dogs; that would have to wait for another day. In the meantime, Louise's feet were killing her. 'Your witty, scintillating company is giving me huge blisters,' she complained. 'So why don't we call it a day and have a few drinks together?'

Clive thought it was a great idea.

In the morning, they set out to count the dogs. 'Is there anything I can do for you?' Clive asked as they headed along the street, keeping an eye open for their first canine statistic. 'Climb Mount Everest, swim an ocean, hang upside down from a tree? What is it they say? The difficult I can do immediately, the impossible may be take a little longer. That's if you're in no hurry.'

They were holding hands. 'You don't have to do the impossible to impress me, Clive,' Louise said. 'But . . . '

Louise sighed. She had become serious again. 'We've got into this so quickly,' she said. 'And it's becoming a little intense. Sometimes I just can't help wondering . . . ' Her voice trailed away.

'Wondering what?' Clive prompted her with a vague sense of apprehension.

'That you rushed into this because I remind you of Linda. I mean, we've both been hurt. Clive. And . . . Are we just trying to soothe the pain a little?'

'I don't think so,' Clive replied slowly. 'And, anyway, what if we are? Wouldn't it be worth it if we could help each other?'

'Of course it would.'

Clive pressed the point. 'I mean, we make each other happy, don't we?'

'Yes.'

'So what sort of idiot is going to throw away happiness when it's offered on a plate?'

'Not me,' Louise said with a laugh.

'Me, neither,' Clive said emphatically, and kissed her.

They walked on. There was still no sign of any dogs. 'You don't really want to count dogs, do you?' Louise asked.

Clive shook his head. 'No.'

They turned and, arm and arm, headed back towards the house.

That evening, while they were having a drink at the Waterhole, Clive asked where she would like to eat. She said she wasn't hungry.

'I am.' Clive leered at her. 'But not for food.'

Louise pulled a face. 'I haven't heard that one for a while,' she said drily.

'I thought it was original.'

Louise laughed. 'Didn't Shakespeare say something like that? About hungering for the food of love?'

'No, no. That was music. "If music be the

food of love, play on.'" He leaned forward and gave her another long smouldering look. 'I think we could just about get a symphony together,' he said. 'Don't you?'

Louise's smile faded. Clive could see that she was slipping back into one of her serious moods. 'Clive, I've told you – I don't want this to get too serious. I . . . I'm not ready for that yet.'

'Who's being serious?' Clive demanded. 'I'm talking fun. A whole night of it.'

'Now you're boasting.'

'Do you want to find out?'

Louise shrugged. 'Why not?'

They clinked their glasses and smiled fondly at each other. Everything went right for them that night. It was perfect – and in the morning Clive made the claim that the day that had just dawned would be even better. 'And tomorrow is going to be completely out of this world,' he announced.

Louise gently chided him. 'You're making plans again.'

'All right,' Clive conceded. 'Since there *is* no tomorrow, then we just have to live for today.'

'Look, I don't like it any more than you do,' Louise said soberly, 'but sooner or later we'll have to face up to reality.'

'This *is* reality,' Clive said, moving to kiss her. 'All I need, anyway.'

Later that morning, as they strolled along the edge of the lake in the park, on their way to the coffee shop, Clive said suddenly: 'It's not too late, you know. I could change my mind about going to work. So . . . how about a drive in the country?'

'No, Clive,' Louise replied firmly.

'All right then.' Clive shrugged. 'Not the country. Look,' he went on earnestly. 'the world is our oyster. We can do anything.'

'Anything?'

Taking out his wallet, Clive studied its meagre contents bleakly. 'Well, as long as it doesn't cost too much.'

'The only place *you're* going,' Louise said with a laugh, 'is back to work at the coffee shop.'

'Why?'

'Because you must.'

'Not at all. We don't have to do anything we don't want to do. And, anyway, I would much rather spend the rest of the day with you.' He stopped on the path and, swinging to face her, stared compellingly into her eyes. 'In fact, I'd much rather spend the rest of my life with you.'

'Please don't.' Louise looked disconcerted. 'We said? Didn't we? We agreed not to rush each other.'

'Sorry.' Clive stared out across the murky lake where there were no ducks or any other form of wild life apart from a few stunted trees and some reeds. A definite must on the Tacky Tour itinerary.

'Besides, you *need* to get to work.'

Clive pouted. 'Boy, that's the last time I have a serious discussion about reality with you.' All the same, he had received the message. He looked a little grim. 'What you're telling me, though, is that I should ease off a little – that's it, isn't it?'

'A little.'

'Is it okay if we kiss?' Clive asked hopefully.

'That's okay.'

Intimately?'

'Hmmm.'

Clive nodded to the brownish water of the lake. 'Like Burt Lancaster and Deborah Kerr in *From Here to Eternity*?'

'There's no surf.'

'We can make our own surf.'

They kissed on the path beside the lake.

'Well, really,' a voice said disapprovingly behind them. Startled, Clive pulled away from Louise and gaped at the pinched and severe features of Mrs Mangel, the local busybody who had chosen just that moment to come across the embracing couple. 'There is a time and place for everything.'

Clive had already recovered his composure. 'That's right,' he said, 'and this is it.' He moved to embrace Louise again, but she avoided him.

'Clive,' she said uncomfortably, with a quick glance at the disapproving Mrs Mangel, who was fixing Clive with a steely stare.

'I would expect it of *you*.' Mrs Mangel nodded towards Clive. 'But this young lady, hopefully, has *some* standards of behaviour.'

'I'm sorry, Mrs Mangel,' Clive said with an air of devilment. 'But I just can't help myself.' Slowly, he began to advance on her. 'Every time I see a beautiful woman, I've just got to take her in my arms.' He leered at Mrs Mangel whose distaste, as she watched him, was now mixed with wariness. He took another couple of steps towards her. 'Has anyone told you, Mrs Mangel that you yourself are a damned attractive woman?'

With an expression now of horror, Mrs Mangel began to back-away from him. 'That's enough of your shenanigans,' she said uncertainly. 'I think you might find you're needed back at the coffee shop. If you can tear yourself away.' Turning on her heel, she marched briskly along the path away from them.

Clive stared after that retreating picture of outrage, then shrugged. 'It looks as though the whole world wants to make me an honest man today,'he muttered. 'I suppose I had better go.'

'Yes, I suppose you had,' Louise said with a laugh.

For a while, Clive was very happy. He was exuberant, he made plans – and if Louise showed that she still had reservations about fully committing herself, he was nevertheless confident that she would come around in time. Time was all that was needed. What he didn't expect was that it would go the other way. He wasn't ready for that. It came as a tremendous shock to him.

'No, Clive. No jokes,please. I need a clear head for what I want to say.'

He had just bought a bag of jelly beans and was trying to pop one into her mouth. She had turned her head away. Clive had popped the jelly bean into his own mouth. Now, from the tone of her voice, he realised she had something important to say to him – and with a sudden thud inside him, he thought he could guess what was about to come.

71

'Clive, we agreed that there would be no strings attached – didn't we? No plans, no commitments.'

'Yes, I know, but . . . I still think it could work out.'

She shook her head sadly. 'I don't think so.'

'Why not?' Clive demanded.

'Because you want so much to be in love with me you've convinced yourself that you are.'

'No, that's not true,' Clive protested in a pained voice.

'You love me because of Linda.'

'Perhaps once. At the beginning, yes. But it's past that now.'

Louise smiled at him across the table in the coffee shop where they were sitting. 'It's been magic, Clive.'

'But why can't we give it a chance?'

'Because it wouldn't work, Clive. I know it wouldn't work.' She reached for his hand. 'I don't believe in love on the rebound, and that's what it would be. You see, I was trying to get over Nick, not start up something else. I've been thinking about it quite a lot, and now I've decided to go back to England.' Her eyes were moist. Clive sat very still and listened to the finality in her voice. 'And it's not just because of you,' she went on. 'Or even Nick. It's just that all the time I was away I've had this picture in my mind of a place called Australia. And since I've been back I've realised it's not the same picture at all. I mean, all my old friends, they've changed, they've got married, they've moved away. Nothing's the same.' She gave him a small, tremulous smile. 'We've had our fun,

Clive. It really *has* been fun. Like I said, it's been magic meeting you. I mean, you're a lunatic, but I've made up my mind.'

'That sounds awfully final,' Clive said miserably.

'It is final, Clive. I'm sorry. And, please, don't try to talk me out of it. You're so good at doing that. I mean, you start talking and everything seems so . . . plausible. And this . . . ' Her voice quavered a little. 'This is hard enough as it is.'

They were on their feet. Louise kissed him lightly on the cheek, then walked quickly out of the coffee shop without looking back. Devastated, Clive watched her until she was out of sight.

Six

If she hadn't had that fight with Lucy; if Lucy hadn't pushed her so that she had fallen and grazed her knee; if she hadn't stormed back into the house in a rage, Vicki Gibbons would not have encountered the intruder. No threat would have been made and she wouldn't have had that nightmare in which she vividly saw the bloody and mutilated corpses of both her parents.

Vicki's parents were both out. She had let herself into the house – and there he was, this strange man in the living room with her father's stamp album. He looked at her in a startled way before recovering his composure.

'Hello,' he said with a quick smile. 'You gave me quite a fright.'

Vicki wasn't frightened – not yet. 'Who are you?' she demanded suspiciously.

'I'm a friend of your daddy's.'

'What are you doing with his stamp album?'

'Oh, just borrowing it,'the man replied unconvincingly. 'He said I could.'

'I don't believe you,' Vicki said grimly. 'He won't let anyone touch it – not even Mum.' She pointed to the still open cabinet drawer from which he had taken it. 'Put it back.'

'Now listen to me, sweetheart.' There was an edge of menace in the man's voice.

Vicki still wasn't frightened. She was determined to save her father's valuable stamp collection. 'You put it back or I'll scream,'she threatened.

Slowly, the intruder replaced the album in the drawer. 'All right,' he drawled as he turned back to face her, 'I'll tell you what. 'I'll make a deal with you. I won't take the album if you won't tell anyone I was here.'

'I will,' Vicki cried. 'I'll tell Dad and Mum, and Uncle Clive.'

The man's face was suddenly a rigid mask. His eyes were narrowed, and he spoke in a low, harsh voice. 'You say one word about me being here, and something very nasty will happen to your mummy and daddy.'

This was when Vicki began to be frightened. 'What do you mean?'

'I mean, I'll come back and kill them,' the intruder said, moving past her to the front door.

Terrified by now at the thought of what he would do to her parents, Vicki stared out through the open front door at the stranger. Glancing quickly up and down the street, he hurried to the car that was parked outside the house. He climbed in, started the engine, then backed the car to clear Tom Ramsay's van which was standing just in front of it. There was a bump and a clatter as the car backed into Lucy's wheelbarrow and crushed it out of shape. Then the car was heading rapidly down the street. Vicki rushed out of the house and stared in dismay at the the mangled remains of the wheelbarrow, the rusty pony that had almost taken on a life and personality of its own, so attached had they become to it. It was the poor pony over which the girls' fight had been in the first place.

She was still staring at it when her mother arrived back with a shopping bag full of groceries. Hugely relieved to see her, Vicki ran up to her. 'Oh Mum, I'm so glad you're back,' she cried, hugging her.

'What happened to your pony?'

'A car hit it.'

'Oh dear,' Kate Gibbons said with a sigh. 'It shouldn't have been on the road in the first place,' she added reproachfully. Taking Vicki by the hand, she began to walk towards the front gate. 'Maybe Daddy or Uncle Clive will fix it. I hope it didn't do too much damage to the car. Do you know who it was?'

'No,' Vicki said quickly. 'I don't know.'

'I'm sure they'll find us if they need to.'

Vicki's heart was racing. 'Yeah,' she breathed, clutching her mother's hand.

After dinner that night, during which she had hardly eaten a thing, Vicki sat huddled up in a corner of the living room sofa, clutching one of her dolls. Her fear worried at her, nagged at her, wouldn't go away. Her mother came out of the kitchen. 'Are you sure you don't have any homework tonight, Vicki?' Vicki nodded listlessly. Kate Gibbons frowned. 'Aren't you feeling very well?' she asked.

'I'm all right,' Vicki murmured.

'Your throat isn't hurting, or anything like that?' Vicki shook her head. Clearly concerned, Kate crossed the room to the sofa where her daughter was sitting so abjectly. 'Sweetheart, I know you're upset about your pony, but honestly, it was really just an old wheelbarrow. If Daddy can't fix it over the weekend, then I'm sure he'll make you something else. Now young lady,' she said with a smile, 'it's off to bed you go.'

'No!' Vicki was suddenly close to panic. She couldn't leave them alone, knowing what she did. There was that man out there, lurking around somewhere, in the shadows, with a knife, watching her to make sure she didn't tell her parents what she had seen that afternoon. 'I want to sleep with you and Dad.'

Kate's eyes widened in surprise. 'Aren't you a little big for that?'

'Please. I'm frightened.'

Kate looked puzzled. 'But there's nothing to be frightened about. Everything's locked up.'

Vicki clutched at the straw. 'Are you sure? All the doors and windows?'

'Of course.' Kate sat down beside her. 'Vicki, what's the matter? What has got into you all of a sudden?' Vicki could say nothing. She could only shake her head. 'Would you like it if Daddy read to you for a while before you fall asleep?'

Coming into the room just then, Graham Gibbons had overheard this. 'Would you mind doing it tonight, darling?' he said to his wife. 'I've got some new stamps I want to put into the album.' Vicki froze. The stamp album. The man had taken the album out of the drawer, and the drawer . . .

77

'That's funny,' Graham said. 'Who left the drawer open?' He turned to his daughter. 'Vicki, have you had my stamp album out?'

'No,' Vicki cried out in alarm. 'I haven't touched it. No one has.' She was quite desperate. It was plain that her father didn't believe her.

'Listen, honey,' he said firmly, 'You know my stamp collection is strictly off limits.'

'But I *didn't* touch it.' Angry tears stung her eyes.

'Don't fuss, Graham,' Kate interceded. 'I probably left the drawer open myself when I was dusting.'

'Oh, well.' Graham looked slightly mollified.

'Vicki's a bit upset tonight,' Kate explained. 'About her pony. And she had a fight with Lucy.'

'What about?'

'Whose turn it was to ride on George.' George was the wrecked pony or rusty wheelbarrow.

'They will soon be forgotten,' Graham observed. 'Right, Vicki?'

Vicki nodded. Her mother said, 'The thing is, she would like to sleep with us tonight.'

Graham grimaced. 'That usually means that none of us gets much sleep,' he murmured wrily.

Vicki began to plead with him. It was so important; it was life and death. While that man was out there . . . 'Please, Daddy. Please.'

Graham glanced uncertainly at Kate who gave him a slight nod of encouragement. He relented. 'All right then,' he said, 'but we're not making a habit of it. Now go and get ready for bed.'

Vicki went to her room and got herself ready for bed, but it was still too early for her parents to retire. They were watching television as she came back into the living room.

'You should be in bed, darling,' her mother said in mild rebuke.

'When are you and Daddy coming to bed?'

Graham rose to his feet. 'When this movie finishes,' he said severely. 'Now you go back to bed, and I don't want to hear another word out of you. We're letting you sleep in our bed, and that's enough.'

'But I want *you* to come to bed, too,' Vicki protested shrilly. She clutched his hand. Her eyes were very wide. 'Please, Daddy. I'm frightened.'

Her parents exchanged a puzzled glance. 'What on earth is wrong with you?' Graham demanded testily.

'Are you homesick, sweetheart?' Kate asked her.

Homesick. Yes, that was an answer. Homesick for the country where she'd had her own pony, the real George she missed so much since they had come to Erinsborough to stay with Uncle Clive until they could move into their own place. How desperately she wished now that her father hadn't given up his medical practice in the country to take up a new one here. 'Yes,' she said hastily. 'I miss George. I want to go back to the country. Please, can't we go home. Please . . . ' She was trying very hard. She was very upset. Graham held her in his arms.

That night, she had a nightmare. She saw her parents' bodies lying on the floor of the living room, their eyes wide and staring and full of horror so that she knew that they were dead. There was blood everywhere, a river of it. She woke up screaming. She was sweating profusely, her heart was pounding; the terror was constricting her.

'What's the matter, darling?' Kate was cradling her in her arms.

Vicki was sobbing. 'I dreamt you were dead. I dreamt the man killed both of you.'

'It's all right.' Kate held her tight as she spoke soothingly to her terrified child. 'It was just a nightmare.'

That morning, after her father had gone to the surgery, Vicki was determined not to let her mother out of her sight. But Kate had things to do. She had a hairdressing appointment, and then after that, some shopping to do. Vicki would be bored. Kate took her to the Robinson house.

'I do appreciate your looking after Vicki this morning,' she said to Helen Daniels.

'That's all right.' Helen beamed pleasantly down at Vicki. 'We get along famously, don't we?' When Vicki remained unresponsive to this, Helen said, 'I'll go and tell Lucy you're here.'

After Helen had left the kitchen in search of Lucy, Vicki made one last plea to her mother. 'Mum, I want to go with you.'

'We've been through it all before, darling. You'll be much better off here.'

And while she was here, anything could be happening. Her mother could be knocked and killed by a hit-and-run driver; she could be pushed under a train . . . 'Please, Mum.'

'No, Vicki. You're staying here. You can make up with Lucy.'

Followed by Helen, Lucy came into the room. She and Vicki were both still a little awkward with each other after their fight. 'I'll leave you to it,' Kate said, kissing Vicki on the forehead, and heading for the door. 'Thanks again, Helen.'

A chilly silence persisted between the two small girls. Helen tried to jolly them out of it. 'Come on, you two. You're not going to be like this all morning, are you? Why don't you go out and play with George?'

'Can't,' Vicki said sullenly. She was thinking of her mother out there, alone and vulnerable. A knife in the back, or a shot in a deserted lane . . .

'Why not?'

'Because Lucy left him on the road, and he got run over.' In the same way as her mother would get run over? She should have gone with her; it didn't matter if she would be bored while she waited at the hairdresser's.

'What?' Lucy exclaimed. 'Poor George!'

'Have you any idea who did it?' Helen asked.

'I didn't see him,' Vicky said with a quick shake of her head.

'Him?'

'I didn't see anybody.' Vicky was on the verge of panic. She began to cry. 'I *didn't*!'

Helen was watching her with a concerned expression. 'Vicki, don't be upset. We'll patch up poor old George.'

81

Lucy came up to Vicki and placed a comforting arm around her shoulder. 'Your dad will. He's a doctor.' The thaw was complete.

'He said he would try,' Vicki told her.

'Come on.' Lucy led her to the door while Helen stared after them with a puzzled expression.

But they couldn't patch up poor old George – and, anyway, Vicki's heart wasn't in it any more. Nor was it in the game of ludo Lucy suggested. After one game, which Lucy won, Vicki didn't want to play any more. 'When is Mum coming back?' she asked Helen.

'Soon, I should imagine.'

'I don't like it,' Vicki said tensely.

'Don't look so worried,' Helen said solicitously. 'There's nothing to be worried about.'

When Lucy suggested they go across to Vicki's place to look through some of her horse books, Vicki almost yelped. She didn't want to go into that house while her parents were not there. 'All right,' Lucy said impatiently. '*You* decide what we can do.'

Vicki knew only too well what she would like to do. 'I wish I was back in the country,' she said wistfully. 'Then I could go for a ride on George – the real George.' The tears welled in her eyes: 'I hate living in the city. Terrible things can happen to you.'

Later, as they were once more mournfully regarding the crumpled George, Lucy asked, 'Who would have done a thing like that? I mean, they would have seen him.'

'He didn't care,' Vicki said without thinking. 'He did it on purpose.'

Lucy looked at her sharply. 'How come you know a man did it? You said you didn't see anybody.'

Vicki made a forlorn attempt to cover the slip she had made. 'But I didn't see anyone.'

'You said he did it on purpose.'

'I didn't say that,' Vicki blustered.

'Yes, you did,' Lucy said accusingly. 'You said you knew he didn't care. George is my horse, too, you know.'

Suddenly, Vicki couldn't hold it back any longer. She had to tell someone: the burden was too great for her to bear alone. 'He said he would hurt Mummy and Daddy if I told anyone.'

'Who?' Lucy was studying her closely.

'This man. He was in the house.'

'But who?'

'I don't know. He wanted to take Daddy's stamps, but I made him put them back. And then he ran over George.' She clutched Lucy's arm. 'You mustn't tell anyone, Lucy,' she implored. 'You must promise.'

'Tell anyone what?' Helen Daniels said from the porch above them.

Vicki's mother was with Helen. Aghast, Vicki stared up at them. How much had they heard? 'Well?' Helen prompted when the two girls remained silent.

'We're not mind-readers, Vicki,' Kate said sternly. 'So come on, what are you two up to?'

Quickly recovering from the shock, Vicki was now thinking fast. 'It was really Lucy's idea.'

'Mine?' Lucy looked startled.

'You remember,' Vicki said, staring at her intently, willing her to go along with her hurriedly improvised story. 'We were talking about the people who ran over George.' She turned back to her mother on the porch. 'We shouldn't let them get away with it, Mum.'

'There's not much we can do about it, darling,' Kate said gently. 'We should be grateful George was only a toy.'

Helen was staring thoughtfully at Lucy. 'So what's the big secret?' she queried.

'Well.' Vicki was still thinking fast. 'Lucy said that the car would have a scratch on it, and the scratch would match George's paintwork – and if we could find the car, we'd know who did it.'

Helen was still watching Lucy with a slight frown. 'That was your idea, was it?' she asked quietly.

Lucy nodded and made a non-committal sound. She was looking rather guilty. 'We weren't going to tell anyone,' Vicki supplied, 'because we thought you wouldn't let us look.'

'Absolutely right, young lady,' Kate said crisply. 'No amateur detective work. You can get into all sorts of trouble that way.'

Vicki and her mother returned to their house for lunch. Although she was to some extent relieved that she and Lucy seemed to have got away with their story, she was still feeling miserable, still trapped by the awesome responsibility of protecting her parents from the stranger who had threatened to kill them if Vicki said one word out of place.

'No one saw who ran over poor George,' Kate said as she began to prepare lunch. 'It was most likely someone using our driveway to turn their car.'

'Maybe.' Vicki only wished her mother would change the subject.

But she was persisting with it. 'If you and Lucy made a mistake and accused the wrong person, it could create a lot of trouble. Don't forget we're new to this neighbourhood. We have to get on with people.'

'I understand, Mum.' Vicki avoided her mother's eye. 'We won't do it.'

'Come here, Vicki,' Kate said quickly. Reluctantly, Vicki moved across to her mother. 'There's something wrong, isn't there?'

Vicki refused to look into her mother's eyes; if she did, she felt that all her resolve would melt away. She wished she didn't feel so helpless. 'What makes you say that?' she murmured uncomfortably.

'Mothers are supposed to know these things. It goes with the job. So?'

'I'm all right.'

Kate was becoming exasperated by her daughter's stubbornness. 'We can't help you with your problems if we don't know what they are, Vicki.'

'There's no problem,' Vicki lied. 'There's nothing wrong with me – honest.'

'Well, if you don't want to talk about it,' Kate said, 'you'd better go and wash your hands for lunch.'

That afternoon, her Uncle Clive had a talk with Vicki. Something was happening, Vicki knew. Her mother had been strangely tight-lipped for the past couple of hours, and when her father had come home, she'd had a quiet word with him about something behind the closed door of their bedroom. Vicki had heard her father swear; he had sounded quite angry. Vicki wondered if it had anything to do with the visit Helen Daniels had made to the house shortly before her mother had become so moody. If it *did* have have anything to do with Mrs Daniels' visit; if she had somehow managed to worm the truth out of Lucy – that would have been the worst thing that could have happened. Vicki was suddenly very frightened again. She had to see Lucy to find out if her fear was justified. But before she could do that, Clive had taken her to one side.

'Now I have to find out what's wrong with you,' he said, 'so I can cheer you up.'

Vicki was very fond of her Uncle Clive; he was crazy, always coming out with funny things. She knew her parents didn't altogether approve of him because he had once been a doctor but had given it up to do nothing much at all. Usually, he could cheer her up; now she wasn't so sure. 'There's nothing wrong,' she murmured.

'Let's talk about that.'

Vicki shifted restlessly. 'I have to see Lucy . . .'

'Come here.'

Hesitantly, Vicki crossed the room to where he was standing. He took her hand. 'Step into my office.' He lowered himself onto the living room carpet, positioning her opposite him.

'I hear you've been having bad dreams,' he said.

Well, there was that one dream where there had been so much blood. Vicki stared down at the carpet in front of her. 'Yes,' she replied almost inaudibly.

'What about?'

'Just bad.'

Clive nodded. 'I guess that fight with Lucy was pretty upsetting,' he remarked.

'It's not Lucy. Lucy's my friend.'

'That's all right then.' He frowned in sudden concern. 'Hey, it's not me, is it?'

'No, of course not, Uncle Clive.'

'Well, that's a relief.' Clive grinned at her, then became serious again. 'Of course, if you're upset because of your Mum and Dad . . . Well, that's no business of mine.'

'It's not Mum and Dad.' Vicki was becoming agitated again. 'It was just a dream, that's all.'

Clive was regarding her shrewdly. 'There's no reason to have bad dreams. There's nothing bad in this house.'

'Bad things can come from outside,' Vicki pointed out to him.

'What kind of things?' Vicki said nothing, but continued to stare at the carpet.

'Vicki,' Clive said gently, 'you'd tell us, wouldn't you, if you knew of something bad?' Vicki was still silent. 'Because if you didn't,' Clive went on after a short pause, 'we'd all be in danger.'

Vicki looked up at him at last. She was being torn apart by what he was saying. She wanted to tell him, desperately, but it was too risky. He reached out and took both her hands. 'Do you trust me?' There were tears in her eyes. She nodded dumbly. 'Do you think I'd let anything bad happen to you?' She shook her head. Of course he wouldn't let anything bad happen to her. 'Or to your Mum and Dad?'

'But you can't stop it.' She began to sob.

'But I can if you tell me, Vic,' Clive said earnestly. 'I promise you that. But only if you tell me. Only you can do that.'

He *knew*. He knew all about it. Lucy, and Mrs Daniels, her angry mother and father – they knew all about it. The tears were really coming down; she couldn't hold them back any more than she could the secret which had been such a fearsome weight for her. 'He was here,' she whimpered. 'He said . . . He said he would . . . Kill Mum and Dad . . . '

Then Clive was holding her in his arms, rocking her gently in his arms as she finally let herself go and her tears moistened the front of his shirt. 'We'll stop him, Vic,' he soothed her. 'No bad things in this house. That's a promise.'

She was feeling a little better when she told her story to the policewoman who came to the house a short while later. There was a policeman with her, but it was the policewoman who gently and patiently extracted the story from her. Vicki told her everything she could remember – about the man she had found in the house with her father's stamp collection under his arm, the threat he had made, and the mangled wheelbarrow.

'If you can think of anything more about this man,' the policewoman said at last, 'you'll tell your Dad, won't you?'

Vicki nodded.

'I'm sorry she couldn't be more accurate,' Graham Gibbons said. 'But you must admit it was a fairly traumatic experience for her.'

'Yes, of course it was.' The policewoman smiled at Vicki. 'You're a brave girl, Vicki. Don't you worry. We'll find him.'

After the police had left the house, Vicki turned apprehensively to her parents. 'Are you mad with me?'

'No,' Graham assured her. 'As a matter of fact, I'm rather proud of you.' He glanced at his wife. 'We both are.'

Vicki was relieved to hear it. 'I didn't know what to do.'

'Well, you do now,' Kate said. 'No more secrets – right?'

'Right.' She hugged them both. She loved them very much – and they were safe now that it was in the hands of the police.

Seven

When Charlene brought the baby home that day and quite calmly announced that it was hers, Madge was horrified. At first, Scott Robinson thought it was a joke. 'Come on, Lennie,' he chuckled. 'Whose baby is it? Really?'

'I told you.' Charlene was rocking the baby in her arms. 'He's mine.'

But Scott was still disbelieving. 'All right, the joke's over. Come on!'

'Believe me, or don't believe me,' Charlene said with a shrug. 'It's up to you.'

'But it can't be!'

'Why not? I told you about the time I got pregnant.'

Madge couldn't forget it. Charlene had come right out with it one day, in the middle of one of their fights. In a rage, she had told her mother about the baby she had been expecting in Coffs Harbour. 'But you said you didn't *have* the baby,' Madge protested weakly.

'Well, I lied,' Charlene returned defiantly. 'I knew I was coming down here to live with you.' Still rocking the baby which was wrapped in a blue shawl, she looked enquiringly up at her mother.

'How would you have felt if I had turned up here with a baby?'

It wasn't a question that Madge could answer. Charlene hadn't turned up with a baby then, but she had turned up with one now – and the only thing Madge could feel right at this moment was total amazement. 'You wanted to know why I was wagging school,' Charlene went on, after a pause during which the tension had grown in the kitchen of the Ramsay house. 'Well, now you know. I wanted to see my baby.'

By now Scott's disbelief had been replaced by bewilderment. 'But if it was such a big secret, how come you've decided to let everyone know about it all of a sudden?'

Charlene glared at him. 'I just *did*,' she snapped. 'Okay?'

'It just doesn't add up,' Scott said with a puzzled shake of his head. 'I . . . Look, Lennie . . . I don't believe you. I don't know why you're trying to tell us that the baby is yours.'

'I've told you the truth,' Charlene said flatly while her mother just continued to stare at her in astonishment. 'I don't see why you're getting so upset about it, anyway. You and I – you've just dropped me, said it was all over between us. What do *you* care if I've got a baby or not?' Turning, she walked out of the room. Scott was about to follow her when Madge stopped him.

'Leave it, Scott.'

Scott looked at her helplessly. 'I just want to know why she's trying to convince us that the baby is hers.'

Madge had already come to accept the truth of what Lennie had just told them; she knew her daughter much better than Scott did. 'She wouldn't bring home a child and pretend it was hers just for the sake of it.'

Scott was still confused. 'Yes, okay, all right – I just want to know the full story. I mean, she *is* my girlfriend.'

'Not according to Charlene,' Madge reminded him.

'I still want to know . . . '

'It's a family matter, Scott,' Madge said evenly. 'Now I suggest you go home. I want to talk to Charlene. Alone.'

Charlene had put the baby to sleep in her bedroom. 'I've always known you were selfish,' Madge said sternly, 'but I never expected this. You materialise a baby out of thin air and then expect me to take it in. No word of explanation. Nothing.'

'I would have warned you if I could,' Charlene muttered. 'But I had to think of something quickly.'

Madge made a rapid and simple calculation. 'You must have been pregnant when I was still in Coffs Harbour.'

'I was. I was too scared to tell you.'

'But I would have noticed. I've got eyes. I wouldn't have missed it.'

'Not until near the end.' Charlene shook her head. 'And you were down here by then. Look, Mum.' She was making a plea for understanding. 'He's *my* baby. I didn't want to give him away. But I knew if I brought him down here you would have

92

had a fit. So I, I found him a foster mother.'

'What makes you think I wouldn't have a fit now?'

'I didn't have any choice,' Charlene told her. 'The foster mother is sick. That's why I've been wagging school. I've been going over to see her. And she's got worse.' She sighed. 'And I couldn't just leave him there. I didn't know what else to do.'

'Well, obviously your father knew about all this,' Madge observed bitterly. 'How come *he* didn't support you both?'

'He had to think of Susan,' Charlene replied hesitantly.

'Oh yes, of course.' Madge's face hardened. 'The girlfriend. I'd forgotten about her. No wonder he threw you out.'

'It wasn't like that,' Charlene protested. 'I didn't want to stay.'

'I'm going to call him,' Madge stated. 'He will *have* to make a financial contribution.' No, there was no way he could evade any responsibility for this. She moved towards the telephone. 'He's got the business, and I've got nothing.'

'There's no point, Mum. He's gone.'

Madge stopped and swung back to face her daughter. 'What do you mean?'

'He's gone. He doesn't live in Coffs Harbour any more.'

Madge was alarmed. 'What about the business?'

'He sold it.'

It was a day of shocks. Madge had put twenty years of her life into that business: she should have received *something* in return for the effort. She didn't know whether to believe Charlene or not. 'Where has he gone?'

'I don't know.'

Madge's eyes narrowed as she studied her daughter. She was always on her father's side; she always stood up for him. 'You probably wouldn't tell me even if you did know.'

'It's true. He didn't say.'

Madge had no choice but to believe her. 'Oh, I might have expected it,' she said in weary resignation. 'He's got no more sense of responsibility than you have. And now he's left me with an unmarried mother – and another mouth to feed.' It was too much. The crosses she'd had to bear in life; there was to be no end of them.

She was still brooding over it as she prepared the dinner. In the other room, the baby woke up and began to cry. 'You'd better bring him out here,' she called sharply to Charlene, who at that very moment appeared in the doorway with the baby in a carry-cot.

'I've brought him.'

Madge had to raise her voice to make herself heard above the noise. 'A baby shouldn't be pushed around from pillar to post,' she said, 'let alone from mother to mother.'

'Then he'd better not be moved again.' Charlene looked hopefully at her mother.

'What about the father? Is *he* doing anything to help?'

'He ran away as soon as he found out I was pregnant. I told you that.'

Yes, she had. Some type *he* had turned out to be. Another one who ran away from his responsibilities. 'Maybe the police will be able to find him.'

'No.' Charlene looked suddenly alarmed. 'I mean, how can they prove who the father is, anyway?'

Madge moved slowly into the living room. Behind her, the baby had stopped crying for the moment. 'I always knew you were wild, Charlene,' she said sadly, 'but I never really thought you would end up as an unmarried mother.'

Charlene placed the carry–cot on the sofa. 'If you won't let him stay,' she said with determination, 'then I'm moving out, too.'

Madge glanced at the baby which was gazing blandly up at her. It was very pink. 'Don't be silly. Where would you both go?'

'I'll find something. I could be a housekeeper, for instance. The ads often say it's all right if you've got a baby.'

'You?' Madge looked at her incredulously. 'A housekeeper?'

Charlene brightened. 'So we can stay then?'

'Charlene, look.' Madge spoke very seriously. 'Have you thought this thing through? Babies are very small, but they cost a lot of money to keep.'

'Then I'll get a job. I want to leave school, anyway.'

'Oh no you don't,' Madge returned emphatically. 'You need your education more than ever now. You have to give him a decent upbringing.' She glanced at the baby again. 'You haven't even told me his name.'

'Frederick Samuel.'

'Frederick . . . ' Named after his grandfather – very nice, very touching. The rat Fred didn't deserve it.

'I call him Sam, though.'

'Sam.' That was better. 'It suits him.'

'Can we stay then?' Charlene asked tentatively.

The baby began to cry again. 'Charlene, I'm not the only one with a say in this. I'll have to ask the others.' She sighed. 'Heaven knows what Tom will say.'

It was a problem that she discussed with Helen Daniels and Paul Robinson when she went next door that evening to give Scott an explanation for her earlier abruptness. 'Of course I can't,' she replied dolefully when Helen asked her if she could afford to look after the baby. 'And now Charlene is threatening to leave school. So *any* hope she had of a decent future will go right out the window.'

'But if she *does* stay at school,' Paul offered, 'that means you will have to look after the baby. That will be a bit hard on you, won't it?'

Madge was well aware of that. 'I won't have time to look for a job,' she said.

'You shouldn't make any decisions until you've had time to talk it over with Tom,' Helen suggested.

Madge knew she was in for a struggle, but the point was, she still wasn't sure what her own attitude was. She wasn't sure at all what would be for the best. She decided it was time to come to the point of her visit – not that that would be much easier. 'Actually, I was looking for Scott,' she said. 'I wanted to have a word with him.'

Helen found Scott and brought him back into the room. Madge was feeling very awkward. She had been so unfair to the boy in the past over his relationship with Charlene; she had really come to apologise. 'Did Lennie tell you everything?' Scott asked her.

Madge nodded. 'Yes, she did. And I think *you* have a right to know as well.'

Scott's face was blank, his manner listless. 'I don't care,' he muttered.

Madge was determined to have her say no matter how difficult she found it. 'It seems the child *is* Charlene's,' she told him. 'She lied to me about having . . . Well, you know. She had the baby after all.' Scott was watching her stonily; Madge wasn't finding this easy. 'I've said things to you in the past. About you and Charlene. I know I haven't been fair. But Charlene . . . It seems she's beyond the point of being able to take charge of her own life. She seems hell–bent on dragging everyone else down with her.'

'Is that right?' Scott's tone was aggressive.

Paul stepped forward. 'She *is* trying to apologise, mate.'

But Scott wasn't to be placated. 'You're all as bad as each other,' he cried angrily. 'Hypocrites. Lousy hypocrites.' He glowered at Madge who was startled by the suddenness and savagery of his attack. There had been bad blood between them in the past, things had been said, but this . . . ' I don't *need* it,' he yelled. 'I don't need her, and I don't need this.' He stormed out of the room.

Tom Ramsay was late home for dinner: he and Shane had been at the pub where they had lost two games of darts. When he saw the baby in its carry–cot, and after having recovered from the shock, he studied it with furrowed brow from one side then from the other. 'If this is some kind of joke, Charlene,' he growled, 'then it's in very poor taste.'

'But it's true, Tom,' Madge insisted. 'It's Charlene's baby. His name is Sam.'

'Well how come we haven't heard about this baby before?' Shane queried.

'I didn't want to upset Mum,' Charlene explained. 'But when the foster mother got sick, I had to bring him here.'

'What about the father? Can't he help?'

'I don't know where he is now.'

Tom clenched his fists. He wasn't in a good mood after his defeat at darts. 'I'll find him,' he said fiercely. 'Make him face up to his responsibilities.'

'No, Tom,' Madge said. 'As Charlene has already said, it would be very difficult to prove he *was* the father.'

'I'll beat it out of him,' Tom muttered. 'Make him confess.'

'Don't be silly, Tom,' Madge chided him. 'No,' she went on with a shake of her head, 'the boy obviously isn't prepared to do anything.'

'There's still something to be said for the old-fashioned shotgun wedding,' Tom opined.

Madge could see no point in carrying on like this. It wasn't helping matters at all. 'The point at issue now,' she said, 'is what do we do with the baby? It's really up to you two. I can't afford to support both of them, so if Sam is to stay, Tom, you'll have to provide some financial support.'

Shane was peering at the baby. He chuckled. 'He's quite cute, really,' he observed. 'He looks like Uncle Fred.' Madge gave him a sharp slap across the back of his head. 'Oops, sorry.'

Charlene was looking steadily at her uncle. 'Please, Uncle Tom,' she implored him. 'There's nowhere else I can take him.'

'Shouldn't be hard,' Shane suggested. 'He doesn't take up much room. And I don't mind chucking in a few extra bucks a week.'

Tom looked from her to the baby. He scratched his head and frowned in perplexity. He sighed. 'I'm damned if I do and I'm damned if I don't.' He looked unhappily at Charlene. 'If I throw you out in the cold, I'll be wicked uncle of the year to everyone in the street here.' He sighed again, and gave the impression of a man very much put upon. 'All right, but I have to say that I'm not exactly thrilled about it.'

'Oh thanks, Uncle Tom,' Charlene cried, hugging him in her delight while the baby gurgled contentedly in its cot.

Madge had almost forgotten what bringing up a baby involved – but she was soon reminded of what a handful it could be. The baby needed to be fed and changed, and put to sleep. He woke them up at all hours of the night. Tom was becoming quite cantankerous. 'It doesn't get any easier,' Madge complained, but she was really becoming quite taken with the idea of looking after little Sam while Charlene was at school.

'Taken a shine to young Fred, haven't you?' Tom said one afternoon.

'His name's Sam,' Madge reminded him coldly. 'Please remember that.'

'Sure, sure,' Tom said hurriedly as he leafed through his notepad. 'Slip of the tongue. But I'm right, aren't I? He's got to you?'

Madge was warming some water for the baby's bottle. 'I'm just looking after the baby while Charlene is at school,' she said crisply. 'There's no more to it than that. My mothering days are behind me, Tom, believe me.'

Tom had just popped in for a few minutes, he had said; there had been something he wanted to check in his pad – he didn't even have time for a cup of tea. 'By the way, are there any messages?' he asked.

'No,' she told him. 'But there's a letter. On the table. It's from Max.'

'Thanks.' He moved across to the table and picked up the letter from his brother.

Madge had been vaguely curious about that letter. It had been addressed to Tom only, and not the whole family as she might have expected. But as she thought about it some more, she decided that one never knew with Max, who had never been predictable. 'Well?' she asked as he skimmed the letter. 'What does he have to say?'

Tom folded the letter. 'Oh, you know,' he said evasively. 'Nothing much.'

It was just this sort of offhandedness that annoyed Madge. 'Oh come on, Tom.'

'Usual stuff,' he said with a shrug. 'Maria's fine, Danny's been up for a visit. Max seems to be doing okay. That's about it.'

Instinctively, Madge knew that that was *not* about it. She had sensed his evasiveness. 'What's going on?' she demanded. 'You two have never been as thick as thieves before.' She tried to pluck Max's letter from his hand, but Tom held it up out of her reach. She knew now that there was definitely something very funny going on.

'Max likes to keep up with the local gossip,' Tom said smoothly. 'You know what he's like'

An awful possibility occurred to Madge. 'Oh Tom, you're not going to tell him about Charlene, are you? Please don't. He'll bust a boiler.'

'Relax.' Tom gave her a reassuring smile. 'We're just pen friends, that's all.' He shoved the letter into the pocket of his overalls. 'Now I've got to go,' he said. 'I'm late.'

Later that afternoon, Madge had a visit from Mrs Mangel. She was very upset by it.

Madge was sitting on the living room sofa, nursing Sam and comparing him with a photograph of Charlene as a baby. She had just decided that there was a stronger resemblance to Fred than there was to his mother, when there was a knock at the front door. She carried the baby out into the hall with her. When she opened the door and saw Mrs Mangel standing there, she groaned inwardly.

'Oh. Hello, Mrs Mangel.'

Mrs Mangel was looking at the baby with an air of disapproval. 'Hello, dear,' she said. 'How are you feeling?' When Madge didn't reply, the older woman made her own quick appraisal. 'I must say you seem to be bearing up remarkably well. This business must be a terrible strain for you.' She smiled rather archly at the baby in Madge's arms.

So the word had got around, Madge thought in dismay: it had filtered through to the sanctimonious Mrs Mangel. 'I'm not sure . . . '

'It's all right, dear,' Mrs Mangel said rather loftily. 'Charlene told me – and frankly, she was quite bold about it. She came to ask me if Janie – that's my granddaughter, you know – if Janie could do some babysitting for her. And of course I asked her whose baby it was.' She frowned at the recollection. 'I was astonished, I can tell you. Such a young girl, and still at school. But,' she continued with a sigh, 'this day and age, the things that go on, moral standards gone by the board, whereas in *my* day . . . ' Her eyes brimmed with compassion as she regarded Madge. 'It must be terrible for you, Mrs Mitchell. I'm sure you must be so disappointed.'

Angered by the woman's patronising tone, Madge sprang to her daughter's defence. 'Mrs Mangel, I will *not* have my daughter spoken about in those terms. Charlene made a mistake, and that's all there is to it.

'A mistake? How charitable of you.'

Madge was forcing herself to remain calm. 'Mrs Mangel, I thank you very much for your concern, but the matter is in hand – and frankly, it does concern the family only.'

Mrs Mangel sniffed. 'I would have thought it also concerned the school,' she said. 'I mean, Charlene will hardly qualify now as a good influence on the other girls, will she? I'm sure Mr White will be more than interested.'

Madge wasn't finding it easy to keep her temper in check. 'This has nothing to do with the school – nor should it.'

'Perhaps it would be best to leave that for others to judge,' Mrs Mangel said imperiously. 'I do know how impressionable young Jane is. Your daughter had the nerve to ask her to babysit. Naturally I put my foot down.'

'And *I'm* about to put *my* foot down,' Madge snapped at her. 'I thank you very much for your visit, but I am very busy.'

Mrs Mangel was taken aback. There was more, apparently, that she wanted to say. 'Yes, but I . . . '

'And if you want to conduct a witch hunt, if you want to persecute my daughter, then that's on your conscience. Frankly, I think she's done a very courageous thing. And I'm sure the school will agree with that. Good day, Mrs Mangel.'

She closed the door very firmly and turned back into the hall. She was shaking with anger.

Charlene was home from school, and Madge was trying to get the baby to sleep, when the telephone rang. Charlene answered it while her mother continued to fuss over the baby. Charlene spoke for only a few moments then hung up.

'Who was that?' Madge asked her.

'Oh, no one important.'

There was evasion written all over her. Madge wasn't pleased. 'More secrets, eh?'

'Mum . . . '

Madge overrode her. 'Now, Charlene,' she said tautly, 'I realise you have to have a life of your own – but isn't this what has caused all the trouble in the first place? Not confiding in me?'

'Please, Mum.' Charlene was looking very tense. 'Don't!'

'I know you're tired,' Madge observed. 'You're tired and wrung out.' Charlene was pale and drawn. 'But it goes with the territory, my girl. It's the price you have to pay.'

There was a deep, welling sadness in Charlene's eyes. 'Can we talk about this later?' she asked in a small voice.

No, they couldn't talk about it later. It had been a very trying day. 'You're not the only one this affects, you know,' Madge said shortly. 'There are other people who know about this. Mrs Mangel, for instance. Do you know she was over here today?'

'Who cares what *that* old gossip says?' Charlene muttered defiantly.

'I do,' Madge cried. 'Sam's not only your son. He's my grandson.'

'Oh, Mum.' Charlene began to sob. She was shaking. 'Please, help me!'

Madge was deeply concerned for her daughter, who looked as if she was in a state of complete exhaustion. She took the girl in her arms and held her close. Then, hearing the baby whimpering in the other room, she released Charlene. She moved out to the cot and picked up the baby. 'Come on, darling,' she murmured. 'Give us a cuddle. There . . . '

Charlene had followed her into the room. 'I'm no different from any other mother,' Madge said to her. 'I've often thought about the time when you would get married and have a family.' She smiled wrily. 'But then you never did do anything by the book, did you?'

'I didn't know it would be like this,' Charlene said woefully.

'No, it's never easy on your own, not at any age,' Madge observed. 'Oh, never mind, love,' she went on more brightly, 'we'll manage. But you have to realise that finding yourself a good job is more important than ever now. So promise me, you will stay with your schoolwork.'

'I will, Mum.'

Madge was still thinking about their future. 'Yes, we'll have to make a fresh start, you and I. But you've got to promise that you will be straight with me from now on.'

Charlene nodded. Madge could see that she was still unhappy. 'Mum, do you mind if I go out for a few minutes?' Charlene asked, after a few moments of silence broken only by the baby's whimpering.

Madge was still rocking the baby gently in her arms and smiling at him. 'Mmm?'

'Just for a walk. It might help clear my head.'

The baby's face puckered, then turned red as he began to yell with all the force of his tiny lungs. 'Yes, all right,' Madge said distractedly as she tried to comfort the child. Then she had a sudden suspicion. 'You're not planning to meet Scott Robinson, are you?'

'I said I would be straight with you.' Charlene eyed her mother reproachfully.

Yes, Madge thought, and her side of the bargain was that she had to start showing some trust in the girl. There had been enough lies in the past, but now a new resolution had been made. 'All right then, dear. I'm sorry. But why don't you dry your eyes and straighten yourself up in case you *do* meet someone you know?'

'Thanks, Mum,' Charlene said, heading for the door and leaving her mother to handle the howling infant.

The baby was finally asleep by the time Tom came back to the house. 'How's it going, Grandma?' he greeted her.

'There's no need to be sarcastic, Tom.'

'Got to face facts, Madge.' He grinned at her. 'I'm a great uncle, and you're a grandma.

We're getting old, Sis.' Rubbing his hands together briskly, he looked around the room. 'Any more calls?' he asked.

'No.' Madge shook her head. 'So you can spend the rest of the day doing your books. They're a disgrace. I don't know how anybody can run a business the way you do.'

'Um . . . I have to do a few things first.'

Like going to the pub and playing darts, Madge thought disapprovingly. 'Oh and by the way,' she said, 'you might find Max's letter while you're about it.'

Tom's face fell. 'I told you what was in it,' he muttered.

Madge regarded him suspiciously. Here was someone else who was being evasive: it was becoming a family epidemic. 'I'm beginning to think you don't want me to read it,' she challenged.

'Don't talk rubbish. Anyway, I've lost it.'

'Well then? Did Max say when he might be coming back?'

'Give a man a break,' Tom said, following her into the living room where she had gone to check the baby. 'He's trying to work things out with Maria.'

'He's had plenty of time to do that.' The baby's eyes were open. Madge knelt down beside the cot. 'Hello, darling,' she cooed.

'Anyway, why do we have to go through all that again?' Tom demanded a little querulously. 'It's probably just as well that Max *does* stay away while we're lumbered with Charlene's baby. I mean, where will he sleep? In the bar?'

107

Madge glanced sharply up at him over her shoulder. 'Would you please keep your voice down. You'll upset the baby. Just take yourself off somewhere, will you?'

'Whatever you say, Grannie.'

'Get out.'

The following afternoon, Charlene answered the telephone again when it rang. 'I have to go out, Mum,' she told Madge after she had finished the call during which she had looked increasingly worried.

'Why?' Despite herself and the new resolution that had been forged between them, Madge was suspicious.

'Barbie, a girl in our class,' Charlene replied awkwardly. 'She gets really upset about second unit maths. I won't be long.'

'Why can't she come over here?' Madge wanted to know. 'You have homework of your own to do.'

'I just told you.' Charlene's voice rose a little. 'She's freaking out. Look, Mum, would you mind looking after Sam while I'm away. I won't be long.'

Madge relented. 'Of course I don't mind. But if you've got schoolwork to do, I expect you back here.'

'I told you, Mum,' Charlene said with an edge to her voice. 'I won't be long.'

All the same, Madge wasn't totally convinced.

She had already begun to crochet a matinée jacket for little Sam, and was working on it when Shane came back into the kitchen after his shower and dumped a pile of dirty clothing in the corner. 'Not on the floor,' Madge commanded. 'Put those things in the laundry.'

Shane began to protest. 'I was going to!'

'There's a child in the house,' Madge sharply reminded him, 'and I won't have him surrounded by your germs.'

Muttering something under his breath, Shane carried the clothes out into the laundry.

Later, while she was doing some tidying around the house, Madge noticed the bundle of clothing in the laundry and decided that she might as well put a wash through the machine. She lifted the bundle, and was about to put it in when she noticed some old letters and papers in the box that had been beneath the clothing. 'What's all this?' she wondered as she began to sort through the box.

'Just some old rubbish,' Tom said quickly, coming into the laundry behind her. 'I'll put it all in the bin.'

But Madge was already rummaging through the old papers. 'I don't think I've been through any of this. Ah!' Her eyes lighted on a familiar envelope. 'Well, well, well.' It was Max's letter to Tom. 'I thought you said you lost it?'

Tom was plainly ill at ease. 'So that's where it got to,' he said weakly. He made a grab for the letter, but Madge ducked out of his way. 'Look, Madge, that's private property. I don't read *your* mail.' He made another unsuccessful grab for it. 'Give it here.'

But Madge was already skimming the letter – and what she read appalled her. She glared at him with a thunderous expression. 'You doublecrossing twisters!' she cried.

Tom began to back away before the onslaught of her mounting fury. 'It's a perfectly sensible arrangement,' he said defensively.

'Oh, is it?' Madge retorted. 'Is it really?' The indignation built up inside her. 'No wonder you didn't want me to read this.'

Tom was trying to calm her down; but he was appealing to a reason that she didn't possess at that moment. 'So Max is taking over my business and my house in Brisbane – and I'm taking over his. Where's the harm in that?'

Harm? 'I'll tell you what the harm is,' Madge shouted. 'Between the two of you, you've cheated me. You're trying to rob me blind.' In the other room, the baby began to cry. Madge shook her head in exasperation. '*Now* look at what you've done,' she wailed.

After she had quietened the baby, the row continued. Madge felt that she was the victim of a vicious conspiracy, even though Tom had just assured her that the whole business was nothing more than a simple technicality. 'Then if it's all just a technicality,' she demanded fiercely, 'why did you two plan the whole thing behind my back?'

Tom was blustering. 'You had your own problems with Lennie. We were trying to do you a favour.'

Two brothers conspiring against their sister – Madge had never heard of anything so outrageous. 'Whoever said blood was thicker than water must have been a single child,' she grated through clenched teeth. They weren't actually yelling at each other at this stage, because Madge was determined not to wake the baby again, but that didn't lessen the intensity of her rage. 'I've never been able to trust either of you.'

Tom was making placatory gestures. 'Listen, Madge, nothing's going to change. No use crying over spilt milk.'

'Just watch me.' Madge pointed a quivering and accusing finger at him. 'I'm not taking this lying down, you know. I'll get legal advice.'

'You'll be wasting your money.'

'We'll see about that.'

'Madge, look . . . ' Tom was still trying to make her see reason. 'We exchanged deeds two days ago. It's already signed, sealed and delivered.'

So it had gone as far as that, had it? A stab in the back. 'You *thieves*.'

'Now, now,' Tom warned her, 'you just watch your tongue. You're not the only one who can get legal advice, you know.'

Madge was about to respond to that when Shane came in through the back door. He stopped when he saw the two belligerents glaring at each other in the kitchen. 'What's going on?'

'What's going on?' Madge retorted harshly. 'I'll tell you what's going on. Thanks to a little deal your father has cooked up, your Uncle Tom here now owns this place. He can now throw us out any time he chooses.'

Shane looked stunned. 'But you can't just swap houses like that!'

'It's legal,' Tom pointed out to him.

Shane glanced uncertainly at Madge. 'But half this house still belongs to Aunt Madge. She loaned Dad the money in the first place.'

Exactly. Madge was grimly triumphant. 'Thank you, Shane.'

'There was only one name on the deed,' Tom informed him, 'and that was your father's.'

'But . . . ' Shane had turned back to Madge again. 'Did you get a written agreement or something?' he queried.

A written . . . They really had her now. She had been far too trusting. 'I didn't think I needed one,' she said lamely.

Charlene came into the room from the hall. 'Mum, I've got to talk to you.'

'Not now,' Madge snapped at her without taking her eyes from that treacherous brother of hers.

'It's urgent,' Charlene insisted.

'For God's sake, Charlene,' Madge cried angrily, 'I'm still trying to find out if we've still got a roof over our heads.'

With an expression of astonishment, Charlene sank onto a chair. 'For crying out loud, Madge,' Tom said in a tone of annoyance, 'no one's throwing *anyone* out.'

'But you could, if you wanted,' Shane rejoined. 'Come on, Uncle Tom, you're the one who's been quoting the law.'

'That's not the point . . . '

'Yes, it is,' Madge broke in. 'And why should I believe you, anyway, Tom?' She was on the verge of tears. 'All I know is that I've been well and truly ripped off.'

112

Tom appealed to Shane. 'It looks as though there's a good chance of your Mum and Dad getting back together again. Max doesn't want to throw that away,' he said to Madge. 'That's why he wants to stay in Brisbane. I fancied a shift down here,' he spread his hands, 'so it seemed a simple solution.'

'Then why have you been keeping it a big secret?' Shane demanded.

Tom glanced uneasily at Madge. 'We thought your aunt would make a fuss.'

A fuss, he called it. 'Little wonder,' Madge snorted. 'You've managed to disinherit Shane, and you robbed me. Why *shouldn't* I make a fuss?'

'Max will pay you back the money he owes you,' Tom told her.

He was being attacked from two sides, while Charlene who had something so important to say to her mother, sat slumped in a chair with her mouth open. 'You two haven't given much thought for the rest of us, have you?' Shane bitterly accused his uncle.

The baby began to cry. Madge lifted him out of the cot and held him out to Charlene. 'Put him in the bedroom.'

'No.'

'What?'

Charlene stared defiantly up at her mother. 'Are you going to listen to me, or not?'

There was something in her tone of voice, a vibrant urgency, that for the first time made them realise that what she had to say to her mother might have been important after all.

'We can finish this discussion outside,' Tom suggested to Shane.

'Yeah, right.'

The tactical withdrawal through the back door completed, Madge turned to her daughter. 'Well, young lady,' she said grimly, 'you've raised your voice, so I hope you have a very good reason.'

'It's Sam.' Charlene was pale but determined.

'What about Sam?'

'He's not my baby.'

Madge stared at her in amazement. 'But that's absurd.'

'I lied to you, Mum,' Charlene said steadily.

Madge was still trying to digest this. She was stunned. 'If it's not . . . ' And then the awful realisation hit her. 'Oh no!'

'It's Susan's baby.'

'Susan's . . . ' Madge felt faint.

'Susan left Coffs Harbour after she broke up with Dad,' Charlene told her. 'She didn't have any choice. Dad was being – well, you know what he's like – and she had to get away. Then she became sick.'

One shock after another. 'How could you do this to me?' Madge groaned. Fred's baby. The girl for whom he had deserted Madge had had his baby, and now that baby was here.

And not only the baby, she saw now to her added dismay, but the mother as well. For Susan was standing in the doorway, swaying on her feet, her eyes hostile in the pallid mask of her face. Madge was furious. 'Get that woman out of here,' she yelled.

'Sam.' The woman in the doorway staggered forward, then with a gasp, collapsed on the floor.

'You'd better get a doctor,' Madge suggested coldly to Charlene as she tried to rouse the unconscious woman.

Charlene straightened. 'I'll get Clive. He knows all about it.'

Madge gaped at her. *Clive* knew all about it? About Susan and the baby? The whole street probably knew by now.

When Clive Gibbons arrived, he swiftly checked Susan's breathing and turned her into the recovery position. 'I believe you knew all about this,' Madge said to him in an accusing tone.

Charlene was holding a glass of water to Susan's lips as she stirred. Clive was checking her pulse. He smiled up at Madge. 'Can I make my excuses later?'

'I doubt if that will make them any more palatable,' Madge remarked drily.

Susan's eyelids fluttered. Her eyes opened. 'How are you feeling?' Clive asked her.

'I'm all right,' Susan replied weakly.

'Tell me what happened.'

'Nothing. I just went a bit . . . funny.'

'What sort of funny? Can you describe it?'

'I fainted, that's all.'

Clive turned to Madge. 'Is there anywhere where I can examine her?'

Madge was feeling extremely put out by all this. 'Is it necessary?'

'Of course it's necessary.'

'Then you'll have to use my bedroom,' Madge said reluctantly.

115

After Charlene and Clive had helped Susan into the bedroom, Madge stood resentfully in the living room. Beside her, in his cot, the baby began to cry. For a moment, she tried to close her ears to the sound. But she couldn't resist it so easily. She picked the baby out of the cot, and holding him her arms, began to make soothing noises. When Charlene returned from the bedroom, Madge held the now quietened baby out to her. 'Here, take him,' she ordered. Charlene hesitated. 'I said, take him,' Madge said bitterly. 'He's nothing to do with me. He's your responsibility now.'

Charlene took the baby. Madge, deeply wounded now that the full implications of her daughter's behaviour had struck home, sat listlessly in an armchair and brooded.

'Mum, I'm sorry. I really am. But I knew if I told you the truth, you wouldn't take little Sam in.'

Madge shook her head sadly. 'I don't understand how you could do that to your own mother.'

'I was desperate.'

'And all for the sake of that floozie.'

'She isn't a floozie,' Charlene protested. 'Listen, Mum, try to understand,' she went on earnestly. 'She . . . Susan helped me when I really needed it. She stood by me when no one else would. And I had to stand by her.'

Madge looked bleakly up at her daughter. 'But haven't *I* ever been good to you? Haven't *I* ever helped you when you needed it?'

'Of course you have.'

'Then why don't you show *me* the same concern?'

'I'm sorry.' Charlene stared defiantly back at her mother. 'But if you hadn't taken little Sam in, he would have been put in a home. And there was no way – no way in the world that I was going to let it happen.'

'No matter who got hurt in the process,' Madge said with a touch of selfpity.

Charlene shrugged and said nothing. Clive came back into the room. 'How is she?' Charlene asked him.

He shook his head grimly. 'Not so good.'

'She's not *infectious*, is she?' Charlene queried in some alarm. 'I mean, she's not dangerous to the baby?'

'Just to herself,' Clive replied. 'She should never have left the hospital.'

'Then I suggest you take her back there,' Madge said sharply.

Clive shook his head again. 'She won't go. I tried to convince her, but she wouldn't listen to me. She won't go without Sam.'

Charlene was shocked. 'But she can't!'

'Why not?' Madge asked.

'Mum!'

'Let her take the baby and go,' Madge said flatly.

'If it was just her, perhaps,' Clive said thoughtfully. 'But she's in no condition to look after Sam.'

'That's her problem.'

'She can have my bed,' Charlene suggested.

'No, she can't.' Madge was adamant. 'She's *not* staying in this house.'

Charlene flared up at her. 'Then if she goes, I go.'

117

'Don't be ridiculous. Where would you go?'

'I'm afraid there's no room at my place at the moment,' Clive said. 'Otherwise . . . '

'She's got to stay here,' Charlene said heatedly. 'There's no choice.'

'No.' Madge's voice was like a whiplash.

'Please, Mum, just for one night.'

'She *is* too sick to move,' Clive said.

The baby whimpered softly in his cot. The baby. No, Madge couldn't throw him out just like that. She sighed heavily. 'All right then,' she relented after a moment's hesitation. 'Just for one night, then that's it. Out they go.'

With a grin of relief, Charlene reached for her mother's hand and squeezed it. 'Thanks, Mum.'

As Madge said to Tom later, she had really hadn't much choice about the matter. The decision had virtually been made for her. Oh yes, she added with a tired smile, she was a real trooper.

The following day was a Sunday. When she was about to leave for church, Madge told Charlene, who was preparing a breakfast tray for Susan, that she wanted Susan and the baby out of the house by the time she returned. She had given in once; she would not give in again.

'Mum, please. Think about it, can't you?'

'No, Charlene, I can't. And I won't discuss the matter any further.'

'But – '

'No.'

'I mean it, if they go, then I'm going, too.'

Madge wasn't fazed by the threat. 'Suit yourself,' she said with a shrug. 'You usually do.'

'I have to, Mum.'

'Then go.'

Sullenly, Charlene picked up the tray and left the room. Tom lowered the Sunday newspaper he had been trying to read during this exchange. 'I think you're making a big mistake, Madge,' he chided her.

'Be quiet, Tom,' Madge snapped back at him. 'Stick your nose in your paper and not my affairs.'

'I was just – '

'I don't care,' Madge interrupted him brusquely. The tension was becoming unbearable. She was almost at breaking point.

'Don't let her go,' Tom said. 'You'll end up like I was in Brisbane. You'll cry "cooee" and you'll hear nothing back.'

Madge eyed him severely. 'You did all right in Brisbane.'

Tom shook his head. 'I had nothing up north.'

'You had a house and a thriving business. That would do most people.'

'But what for?' Tom countered quietly. 'I kept myself busy all day, but then I had to go home to a cold and empty house. And what's the point of that? Why bust a gut when there's no one to share it? Down here, at least, I've got a family.'

Madge could feel herself being backed into a corner. 'I will not have Susan under my roof a moment longer,' she said tightly. 'She has to go, and if Charlene is stupid enough to go with her, then so be it.' And that, she thought, as she picked up her bag and headed out to the hall, was final. There would be no more arguments. She had made her stand, and if they didn't like it, then that was too bad.

But in church that morning, she received a shock. Until the moment the clergyman had uttered those fateful words she had remained quite firm in her resolve. But when she heard the words – devastating in their simplicity – she experienced a wounding pang. It was as if a knife had been twisted inside her. Sitting bolt upright on her pew, the colour draining from her face, she stared at the clergyman, then up at the stained glass windows. There, gazing down at her with compassion, was a mother and a child – another mother, another child. In a fright, she glanced around at the congregation – and it seemed to her that they were staring back at her with accusing eyes. A mother and a child. 'Let those who are without sin cast the first stone.' Those words echoed and reverberated throughout the building. 'The first stone. That's what our Lord said.' Madge shook her head as if to clear it. And the minister was still talking, quietly and earnestly, his damning words piercing Madge with a thousand thrusts.

'Jesus forgave the harlot – and who are we to do less? It is up to us to pick up our own wayward sister and give her another chance.' Involuntarily, Madge's eyes lifted to the stained glass window again, where the mother and child were still gazing down at her with compassion.

She hurried home from church that morning. Susan and the baby were still there. 'Save your breath, Mum,' Charlene greeted her sourly, 'we're just leaving.'

They were in the hall. Clive Gibbons was with them, supporting Susan who was still looking very pale. Charlene was carrying the cot with the baby. 'You don't have to go,' Madge told them in a voice that was shaking a little. 'You can stay here.'

Charlene, who had just pushed past her to the front door, turned back with an expression of surprise. Clive grinned. 'Oh, Madge, I knew you'd come good . . .'

Madge was addressing Susan. 'You can stay until you're well enough to be on your own,' she said with forced determination. 'And not a moment longer.'

Charlene was staring at her in disbelief. Pulling herself away from Clive, Susan took an uncertain step towards Madge. 'Thank you,' she breathed.

'I'm only doing it for the baby's sake,' Madge told her. 'Not yours. And I hope I don't live to regret it.'

Eight

Originally, Eileen Clarke had agreed to look after the coffee shop for just the one day, during the absence of Daphne and her son, Des, the newlyweds. It was a favour to Clive Gibbons, who was supposed to be in charge, but who wanted that day off for romantic reasons of his own.

Then Eileen decided that she liked the work and wanted to stay on, and the problems began.

'Don't get me wrong,' Clive said uncomfortably. 'I mean, your help has been invaluable. It's just that the original arrangement was only for the one day.'

'But I thought it was such a success,' Eileen insisted. 'I mean, the way I dealt with some of the more . . . undesirable customers.' In fact, she was quite proud of the way she had dealt with them: she had brooked no nonsense whatsoever.

'She means the kids from school,' Mike Young told Clive glumly.

Eileen smiled at the memory of her success with the unruly customers. 'Lounging around the place, using bad language . . . '

'But they're our *customers*, Eileen,' Clive protested.

'Customers like *that* we do not need,' Eileen said smugly.

Clive thought about this for a moment. He caught Mike's eye. Mike shrugged. He was only there to do his job. 'Well, all right then,' Clive said finally. 'Give it another day – see how we go.'

'Fine.' Eileen was pleased that he had seen sense at last. 'Decent people will flock in when they realise.' There would be a different class of clientele altogether.

'But Daphne will be back soon.'

'Absolutely. Absolutely.'

When the kids came in at lunch time and started playing the juke box, Eileen found the noise intolerable. She was finding it difficult enough to concentrate on the sandwiches and sausage rolls and milk shakes, none of which could possibly be good for them. She switched off the juke box. 'Some of us would like a little peace and quiet,' she said huffily. 'This is a coffee shop, not a rock and roll venue.'

Scott Robinson began to protest. 'Come on, Mrs Clarke, be fair. We can't even hear it now.'

'Neither can I,' Eileen said emphatically, 'which is the whole point of the exercise.'

She was constantly on the alert for slack behaviour. She looked on disapprovingly as these teenagers, boys and girls, draped themselves around each other. 'Enough of that,' she commanded. 'Sit up straight, if you don't mind. This is a coffee shop, you know.'

'Aw, come off it.'

'Now, no cheek from you, young man. When I was your age . . .'

'Oh come, on, let's get out of here.'

'I think that's a very good idea. Off you go. We don't need your kind in here.'

'Don't worry, we won't be coming back.'

The unruly element was quickly being weeded out. 'Young people these days,' Eileen snorted in disgust. 'They need a lesson in manners.'

'They just want to relax and have fun after school. They don't want someone breathing down their neck,' Mike commented in a strained tone.

'I was doing nothing of the kind, Michael,' Eileen said with impressive dignity. 'Young people lounging over each other like that, and over the tables – it's quite unsightly. If they intend to come in here, they'll have to learn to respect themselves – and each other.'

'Maybe that's why they've stopped coming in,' Mike observed.

When Clive arrived some time later, there were no customers in the place at all. 'Seems a bit quiet for this time of day,' he remarked.

'Oh, everything's going perfectly,' Eileen breezily assured him. 'Smooth sailing.'

'That's what they said on the Titanic,' Clive reminded her gloomily.

There was rebellion in the air. Mike became distinctly uneasy when three teenagers, two boys and a girl, walked purposefully into the still-deserted coffee shop. 'Oh great,' he groaned. 'Just what we need.'

Eileen was bustling forward with a welcoming smile. 'What would you like?' she greeted the newcomers.

'Some information,' one of the youths, a rather gangling creature with a prominent adam's apple and a determined expression, told her. 'I'm thinking of writing an article on this place.'

Eileen was interested. 'An article?'

Mike stepped forward. 'Mrs Clarke, this is John Green, the editor of our school newspaper.'

Eileen beamed at the editor of the school newspaper. 'You must be a very intelligent young man.' He looked at her stonily and said nothing. 'Yes, I think an article in your school newspaper would be a wonderful idea,' Eileen continued.

'You mightn't think it's so wonderful when you read it,' John Green said nastily. 'Are you the old bat who has been getting up everyone's nose?'

Eileen gasped. 'I beg your pardon.'

'Lay off, Greenie,' Mike muttered warningly.

Eileen was still shocked. 'Young man, you'd better leave.' She pointed to the door. 'I *won't* be talked to in that way.'

John Green and his two cohorts didn't move. 'You've been getting stuck into my friends,' he said flatly, 'and I don't like it.' He looked rather superciliously around at the empty tables with their checkered tablecloths, and at the now mute juke box. 'This place used to be all right, until you took over. Now it's the pits. I think it's time I put it out of business.'

Eileen was appalled. What was this self-assured *arrogant* young man telling her? Put the coffee shop out of business? How? 'What do you mean?'

John Green smirked. 'Just you wait and see.' Followed by his two friends he walked to the door. In the doorway, he turned back to Eileen. 'You're going to be very sorry for the way you've treated the kids.'

It was monstrous. The way some young people could *talk* to her! 'Hell,' Mike muttered.

Eileen quickly pulled herself together. 'Well, I won't be daunted by the threats of some young hooligan,' she vowed. 'Anyway, what can *he* do?'

'Quite a bit,' Mike assured her unhappily. 'He's got enough influence over the other guys. And he's into leading causes – save the whales, peace, conservation . . . ' This was awful. Eileen listened to him with growing consternation. 'It's not really conservation he's on about this time, though,' Mike continued. 'I don't think he wants to conserve the coffee shop. Just the opposite, in fact.'

'But he's only a schoolboy,' Eileen pointed out to him.

'Most of our customers are schoolkids,' Mike reminded her.

He was right, of course. 'Oh dear,' Eileen groaned.

The following morning, when Eileen and Mike turned up to open the coffee shop, they were shocked to see that there was a picket line formed up outside it, a line of kids marching up and down, some of them carrying crudely lettered signs. Eileen was outraged. She spotted the obnoxious Green in the vanguard of the demonstration. 'The *nerve* of that young hooligan,' she cried. 'After I expressly told him to stay away.' She marched up to him. 'I should take the broom handle to you!' With a superior smile, the school conservationist turned his back to her and drifted in the opposite direction, followed by his supporters. 'Hooligans,' Eileen muttered again as

126

she unlocked the door of the coffee shop. It looked like the turnover would be even lower than that of the day before.

The picket line was still there when Clive arrived. 'I know just what to do,' he said after he had taken in the situation.

'Oh dear, it's not another of your brainwaves, is it?' Mike said unenthusiastically.

'Oh ye of little faith. Just trust me.'

The solution to the problem had been quite simple, really, he told them later, after the picket line had mysteriously evaporated. 'The first rule of marketing strategy. Everyone will sell out if the price is right and they're beginning to get bored. So I paid them each five bucks to go away.'

That was one problem easily solved. The one that resulted from Eileen's decision to put her home-made salmon mousse on the menu almost created wholesale panic in the neighbourhood.

Des and Daphne were back again. They had been appalled by the damage to the business that had occurred while they were away. Daphne had vowed never to let her mother-in-law loose in the shop again, but when she fell ill (Eileen was convinced she was pregnant – Des said it was just the flu) Des found he had no alternative but to ask Eileen to help out until such time as Daphne was better again.

The place needed variety, Eileen decided, if it was to get back onto a proper footing. A few home-made delicacies would go down well, she thought. The honey touch – people always appreciated that. A mousse perhaps. Avocado? No, there was not enough of that. Salmon? Ah yes, there was plenty of salmon left over in the refrigerator.

Mike was doubtful. 'We'd better throw that out.'

'Nonsense.' Eileen opened the plastic container and sniffed the salmon. 'There's nothing wrong with it.' She emptied the contents into a plastic container. 'All these leftovers should be put to good use. Such a waste otherwise.'

Salmon mousse – Eileen didn't know why she hadn't thought of it before. Just the ticket, she thought happily as she began to prepare it.

By the time they were ready to close the shop, she had made three dozen of them. The mousses sat waiting in the refrigerator in their individual moulds, ready to be presented to an appreciative clientele on the next day of business. She brought one of the moulds out into the shop to find Mrs Mangel had just entered.

'Ah, Mrs Mangel, here to witness my culinary triumph, are we?'

Mrs Mangel looked disdainfully at the mould which was being flourished under her nose. 'What is it?'

Slightly miffed by this lack of response, Eileen said, 'Salmon mousse – what else?' She turned to Des, who was sweeping the floor and looking quite frazzled. 'There are three dozen more setting in the fridge for tomorrow. The customers will love them.'

'Yeah, great, Mum,' Des said with a decided lack of enthusiasm.

Eileen handed him the mousse. 'This is for Daphne. With my love. Just the thing she needs for her condition.'

Mrs Mangel picked up on this. 'What condition?'

Eileen smiled at her in a conspiratorial way. 'Just between you and me, Mrs Mangel, I think I'm soon to be a grandmother.'

Des propped the broom against the wall. 'How many times do I have to tell you, Mum?' he asked wearily. 'Daphne has the flu.'

'Think what you wish, Desmond. Mothers know these things.' Eileen smiled at him knowingly. 'Give her the mousse. It won't upset her.'

Mrs Mangel nodded to the mousse Des was holding. 'Could you spare another three of those, Mrs Clarke?' she asked Eileen. 'They look just the thing for dinner tonight.'

'My pleasure, Mrs Mangel,' Eileen beamed at her. 'Of course, they're not quite set, but if you hurry home and pop them in the fridge . . .'

'Yes, served with a nice side salad,' Mrs Mangel was musing. 'Thank you, Mrs Clarke.'

Eileen turned back to the kitchen. 'My mousse will put this shop on the map, Des,' she chirped happily. 'Just you wait and see.'

In the kitchen she took three of the mousses from the refrigerator and wrapped them in clear Cellophane. 'I'll take them,' Mike offered. 'You finish cleaning up.'

'Thank you, Mike.'

Humming to herself, Eileen began to tidy things away. Noticing that there was a small amount of the mousse mixture left in the bowl, she scraped it into a small plastic dish which she took to the back door. She opened the door. 'Puss, puss, puss,' she called. 'Here, pussy. I've got something very nice for you.'

They weren't exactly clamouring for her salmon mousse, Eileen discovered to her disappointment the following day; even though she did try to promote it as much as she could. 'Mum, I said quiche,' Des said in exasperation, pushing the mousse she had just passed out to him back through the servery.

'But, Desmond, I'm sure the customer would *prefer* my salmon mousse.'

'It's on the menu. He would have ordered it if he wanted it.'

Des wasn't being at all co-operative about this. 'You have to tell him how *good* it is,' Eileen persisted. 'People in here are used to the same boring old food. Anyway, how do they *know* what's good if they haven't tried it?'

'Just give me the quiche, Mum.'

'But what have you got against my mousse? Daphne liked it, didn't she?' When Des didn't answer, she felt vindicated. 'There you are, you see,' she said with a note of triumph. 'Now you just take this plate over to the gentleman and explain . . . Ah, Mrs Mangel, how are you?'

Mrs Mangel was at the counter, looking pale and annoyed, her fingers drumming impatiently on the glass. 'Do *all* your customers have to wait five minutes before being noticed?' she demanded.

Des hurried across to her. 'Sorry. What would you like?'

'A glass of water. Iced. Not from the tap. I feel quite off-colour today.'

Des turned to Eileen who was still at the servery, and who now flashed one of her brilliant smiles at

Mrs Mangel. 'And how did you enjoy my salmon mousse last night?' she asked.

'Very nice,' Mrs Mangel returned grudgingly, 'I must say.'

'And Len? And little Jane?'

'They didn't have any.' Eileen's smile faded just a fraction. 'But nothing was wasted, I assure you, Mrs Clarke. Your mousse is the only thing I've been able to digest since I began to feel ill.'

'Best thing there is for an upset stomach,' Eileen observed sagely.

Des returned from one of the tables. 'Where's the meat pie and chips I ordered? The lady's beginning to complain.'

Eileen passed out a plate of mousse and salad. 'I'm sure she would much prefer this.'

'I'm still waiting for my iced water,' Mrs Mangel said testily.

Des had obviously come to the end of his patience. 'Look, Mum, are you going to cook what the people order? Or do I have to come into the kitchen and do it myself?'

Eileen thought it was a brilliant idea. 'Yes, do that, Desmond,' she said brightly. 'You cook and I'll take the orders.'

Before he could argue about it, she had scuttled out through the kitchen door, and taking up an order pad from the counter, was making a beeline towards one of the tables. 'So sorry about the wait,' she said, poising pencil over pad. 'Now can I draw your attention to the special of the day? An excellent salmon mousse!'

When they came into the shop, she persuaded Helen Daniels and Madge Mitchell to sample the salmon. Helen tasted it. 'Very nice,' she decided. 'What's in it beside salmon?'

Eileen waggled a finger. 'Now that would be telling.'

Scott Robinson ordered salmon mousse when he came in with Charlene Mitchell. 'A very sensible choice,' Eileen said approvingly. 'Charlene?'

'I don't like fish.'

Eileen frowned at her. 'That's because you don't know what's good for you.'

'We live in a wasteful society,' she said rather breathlessly a little later to Mike as they manhandled two large bags of rubbish from the kitchen into the laneway outside. 'People just don't stop to think that the food they leave on their plates could feed the starving children in Africa.'

'At least they ate your salmon mousse without complaint,' Mike observed.

'Yes, they did, didn't they?' Eileen said proudly. 'I'll have to make some more.'

They dragged the bags to the large metal container at the end of the lane. It was full, and a number of garbage bags were propped up against it. One had fallen on its side. 'See what I mean?' Eileen pointed to the bags. 'Sheer waste. Aaaagh, a rat.' Dropping the bag, she jumped back.

There was something sticking out of the bag that had fallen on its side – something long and furry. Puzzled, Mike moved forward and peered at it. 'It's a cat,' he announced. 'Or part of one, anyway. Its tail.' He continued to examine it while Eileen hovered nervously in the background. 'It's Neddy,' Mike stated at last. 'You know, the old stray that was always hanging around. He's dead. Someone must have found him and dumped him there.'

'Oh, poor thing.' Eileen had become quite attached to that cat.

Des came up behind them with another bag of rubbish. 'What's up?'

Eileen pointed to Neddy's protruding tail. 'It's Neddy,' Mike explained.

Des had a look. 'Ah, so it is. I guess I wasn't the only one who didn't like him hanging around.'

'Maybe he died of old age,' Mike suggested.

'Looks pretty bloated to me, ' Des observed. 'I reckon someone has poisoned him.'

Eileen was shocked. 'Oh, how dreadful,' she exclaimed. 'How could anybody *do* such a thing? We were getting to be such good friends. You know, he would come to the kitchen door and wait for the scraps.' She sighed; it was really very upsetting. 'At least, I know he had one decent last meal . . . '

'Wait a minute.' Des rounded on her. '*When* did you feed him?'

'Why . . . ' Eileen thought about it. 'Last night. I gave him some of the leftover salmon mousse.'

Des and Mike exchanged a quick, worried glance. 'That's all the time it takes for a cat to die of food poisoning,' Des said grimly.

'And Mrs Mangel has been off-colour since last night,' Mike supplied. '*She* had mousse for dinner.'

The significance of what they were saying began to sink in. Eileen was horrified. 'But that's ridiculous. Do you realise what you're saying? It's . . . absurd.'

Des shook his head. 'It *has* to be. There's no other answer.'

'I *told* you not to use that stuff in the fridge,' Mike reproached her. 'It was there for days.'

'Oh, fiddlesticks.' It was impossible, quite out of the question. 'It *couldn't* have been my salmon mousse.'

By now Des was looking quite ill himself. 'Do you realise that we sold twenty-six mousses today?' he said in a doom-laden voice. 'And we have one extremely dead cat. Think about it.'

Eileen didn't need to think about it. She was quite convinced it had nothing to do with her salmon mousse.

Des stormed back into the kitchen. Eileen and Mike followed him. 'That salmon *must* have been off,' Des cried desperately.

'Nonsense.' Eileen wished he wouldn't keep attacking her salmon mousse like this. 'That salmon was perfectly all right.'

'Mike said it had been in the fridge for days.'

Mike nodded in confirmation of this. 'Daphne would have thrown it out if she had any doubts,' Eileen said defensively. 'And stop trying to make me feel like a criminal. If that salmon had been off, people would have noticed. And not one customer complained.'

'Who ate it?' Des asked grimly.

'I don't know.'

'You must have *some* idea.'

His anxiety was beginning to rattle Eileen. 'Ah, let me see. You took one home to Daphne . . . '

Des gave a strangled yelp. 'But she didn't eat it. She said she would leave it until . . . Oh my God, I've left her at home with a poisoned mousse.' He ran to the telephone.

Eileen stamped her foot in annoyance. 'Oh really.' Such a fuss.

Des was dialling. 'We'd better make a start,' Mike said urgently to Eileen, 'if we've got to find all those people.'

'Of course we don't. It's just a big fuss about nothing.'

'But what if?'

'It'll be all right. Don't you worry.'

Des came away from the telephone. He was close to panic. 'No answer,' he groaned, running his hands distractedly through his hair. 'She's probably lying on the kitchen floor.'

'Don't be silly, Desmond.'

'I've got to find out.' As he ran to the door, he glared at his mother. 'She'd better be all right.'

'Oh, for goodness sake.'

Within half an hour, Des was back again. Clutching a plastic bag, he dashed into the kitchen just as Eileen was about to emerge with a customer's order. 'I got it,' he muttered.

'Daphne's all right, I presume,' Eileen said tartly.

'A virus. She was seeing Clive Gibbons when I called. He said – ' He saw what she had on the tray. '*Mousse?*' he yelped. 'You can't serve *that*.'

'Of course I can.'

135

'What are you trying to do?' he hissed, thrusting his face close to her own. 'Are you some sort of mass murderer, for heaven's sake? Here.' He grabbed the tray and tried to pull it away from her. Eileen resisted him.

'No,' Eileen cried.

'Yes.'

A small tug-of-war ensued before Eileen finally relinquished the tray. 'Oh, all right,' she said in disgust. 'I'll throw it out.'

'This, too.' Des dropped the plastic bag he was clutching on to the tray. 'It's the mousse I took home for Daphne. She only had one spoonful. She didn't like it.' He gestured towards the kitchen. 'And get rid of any more you've got in there.'

'Then you'd better explain it to the customer.' Eileen stalked back into the kitchen in high dudgeon.

She could hear him apologising to the customer who had ordered salmon mousse, and thanks to him, was not getting it. 'Sorry about that, but the salmon's off . . . No, I mean . . . It's not good enough. The mousse. High standards here, you know. What would you like? Sandwiches? A cup of tea?'

He caught up with her again at the coffee machine. 'Did you get rid of it?'

'Waste of good food,' Eileen replied. 'There's no proof.'

'Better than poisoning people. You should never have used that salmon.'

'I was trying to save you money.'

136

'What? Fifty cents? A dollar? For that you'd risk lives, ruin the business? Daphne's going to kill me. You, too.'

'Nonsense.'

'So what do we do? Try and find the customers and warn them? Or just wait and see?' He groaned. 'Oh, what does it matter? Either way we'll lose the lot. Frightened off, or dead.'

'Don't be ridiculous,' Eileen said sharply under her breath. 'Just bury the cat and forget about it.'

'Get rid of the evidence, you mean?'

'The garbage collection is not for two days. It will start to smell.'

'Oh, right.' He looked at her with sudden hope. 'Do you think we can keep it quiet?'

'I don't see why not,' Eileen replied. 'As long as Mrs Mangel doesn't find out. You know what she's like. And she *did* eat the mousse last night.'

'She'll get poisoned just to spite us,' Des said woefully. 'Oh, brilliant. Just brilliant.'

Mike came back from school while Des was still out burying the cat. 'Where's Des?' he asked.

Eileen had just served milkshakes to four lolling schoolkids whose manners left much to be desired. 'Delivering a package.'

'Eh?'

'Neddy. Gone to his rest.'

She began to clear a table that had just been vacated. Mike followed her. 'I don't get it.'

Eileen hissed at him. 'Burying the cat.'

'Oh.'

Des came into the shop. He looked flustered. 'If I'm charged as an accessory, *you're* paying the lawyer.'

'Sssh.' Eileen indicated the four lolling teenagers.

'Any news?' Mike asked. 'Anyone . . . ?'

Des began acting the clown. He grabbed his own throat, made his eyes bulge, stuck his tongue out. Eileen snapped at him. 'Stop that.' She turned back to Mike. 'Of course not.'

'So far,' Des remarked.

They were in a huddle near the coffee machine. 'What are you guys up to?' Charlene Mitchell asked as she came in with Scott.

They broke apart. 'Nothing,' Eileen said with a guilty expression.

'So what's the big secret?' Scott was looking at them quizzically.

'Just business,' Des replied evasively.

'Big drama at school,' Charlene said to Mike. 'You wouldn't know because you left early.'

'Know what?'

'Mr Mangel came to collect Jane. Apparently, Mrs Mangel was rushed to hospital. Sounds like it could be serious.'

The three of them – Eileen, Mike and Des – stared at her in horror.

'Why don't we ring the hospital and ask what's wrong with Mrs Mangel?' Mike suggested later that afternoon, after Des had gone out to dig the cat up again and take it to the local vet for a post-mortem examination.

'They wouldn't tell us,' Des said. 'We're not family. No, we'll just have to wait until the vet rings his report through.'

They were on tenterhooks. When Eileen tried to take over the coffee machine, Des pushed her away. 'Don't touch,' he said in agitation. 'We're in enough trouble. The business in ruins, the deaths of innocent people hanging over our heads . . . '

'Nonsense. No one has died, and no one will.'

'There's Neddy,' Des reminded her.

'And Mrs Mangel,' Mike solemnly supplied.

Eileen wasn't as sure as she had been. 'She's not a young woman. It could be anything,' she said uncertainly.

The telephone rang. The three of them jumped. Des rushed to answer it. A few minutes later, he rejoined them. He looked relieved.

'The vet said natural causes,' he announced. 'Not a trace of ptomaine, botulism . . . Nothing.'

'Thank goodness for that,' Eileen said with a sigh of relief.

'Died of old age – nothing else.'

'What did I say?' Eileen felt totally vindicated. 'That salmon was quite all right. I can tell when something's off.' She shook her head regretfully. 'And all that mousse wasted for nothing. I'm going to make another batch.'

'Don't you dare,' Des warned her darkly.

'We still don't know what's wrong with Mrs Mangel,' Mike reminded them.

When Mrs Mangel's granddaughter Jane came into the shop, Eileen pounced on her. 'I'm terribly sorry to hear the news,' she said, full of sympathy. 'Is there anything we can do?'

'I was looking for Scott and Charlene.'

'They've gone,' Mike told her.

'How's your grandmother?' Des asked her anxiously.

'I haven't seen her yet,' Jane replied. 'She's still unconscious. They said if she hadn't got to the hospital,' she shrugged eloquently, 'who knows?'

This sounded terrible. Des was looking quite pale. 'Oh dear,' Eileen said with a sorrowful shake of her head.

'But she had the operation just in time.'

'Operation?' Eileen queried faintly.

'Yes, and she's going to be all right.'

'Oh, thank goodness for that.'

'But did they say what it was?' Des wanted to know. 'I mean, how long before they know?'

'They knew straightaway,' Jane told him. 'It was appendicitis.'

'What?'

'Appendicitis.'

'Oh, isn't that wonderful,' Eileen said, and she and Des began to laugh in profound relief while Mrs Mangel's granddaughter looked at them in quite a mystified way.